Beyond the Pale

Hypocrisy & Reality

Book:1

fiction

by

'*Videh*' Arvind Kumar

1957 to 1961

(a novel)

(unlettered)

(*Maar-Haraa, Kunwarpur*)

Dedication

Beyond the Pale
(Hypocrisy & Reality:
Book 1)

Dedicated to the memory of my temperamental father with whom I had a relationship of love and hate both: and it was reciprocal!

Table of Contents

Copyright

Beyond the Pale
(Hypocrisy & Reality:
Book 1)
First published in July, 2024
All rights reserved
@ *'Videh' Arvind Kumar*
Lucknow, India

The right of *'Videh' Arvind Kumar* to be identified as author and publisher of this work has been asserted in accordance with the Copyright, Design and Patents Act.

This is a work of fiction. The names and characters and events portrayed in this book are fictitious and the product of the author's imagination and any resemblance or similarity to real or actual persons, living or dead, is entirely coincidental and not intended by the author or publisher.

Preface

'Beyond the Pale' of Time & Space is the first volume of the fiction series 'Hypocrisy & Reality' and as the name suggests, it deals with the timespan in the life of the protagonist when one had not even had a tryst with the concepts of Time and Space, nor did they make any difference in one's life if those ubiquitous phenomena were not taken cognizance of. Those were the years before the realm of schooling, the arena of perfect unconcern for the written letters, words, or numbers. 'Hypocrisy & Reality' is a fiction series comprising multiple books – novels. The fiction is aimed at depicting the hypocrisy of human society in every respect, be it the upbringing and treatment of babies, toddlers, children, adolescents, youths or the treatment of adults, elders, strangers *et al.*

'Videh' Arvind Kumar
Aashrum, Lucknow, UP, India
July, 2024

Transcripts of *Hindee* letters and *maatraas*

Keeping in view the special pronunciations of *Sanskrit* words, and with a view to differentiating between the disparate pronunciations, we have followed the following regimen of transcription from *Devnaagaree* to Roman script. This clarification will help the readers appreciate the nuances of linguistic specificities and enjoy the text in truly desired sense. Moreover, the vernacular words, particularly nouns, have been italicized.

अ a, आ aa, इ i, ई ee, उ u, ऊ oo, ऋ ri, ए e, ऐ ai, ओ o, औ ऑ au, अं an, अ: :,
क ka, का kaa, कि ki, की kee, कु ku, कू koo, कृ kri, के ke, कै kai, को ko, कौ kau, कं kan, कः kah;

1. About Whom And For Whom?

Enter Protagonist

I must start writing now. It's already too late, 64 years too late. I have all along been harbouring the craving for 'writing': whatever I feel, whatever I experience and whatever I come to know about.

But in this seemingly innocuous pursuit, too, there have been umpteen number of hurdles and hindrances and obstructions created by those closely associated with me: to 'writing', or to unhindered writing.

All — literally all — associated with me have all along been busy creating hurdles in my way of writing or discouraging me: right from that mad and heady authority called father, down to that ingenious prodigy called brother, with others in between. All of them were against my pursuit of writing, particularly, my writing about their veritable characters and hypocrisies, about the truths about them they did not like others to know: of their rudeness, of their insolence, of their indolence, of their misdeeds verging on domestic violence. Also, of their lack of abilities in arranging basic necessities of living, like, *Rotee, Kapdaa* and *Makaan.* Or their lack of common-sense whereby they got entrapped in debts that they kept on borrowing at exorbitant rates of interest from unscrupulous usurers who, invariably in the garb of being their well-wishers, had all along been successful in fleecing them.

The foolhardiness on their part came to an end only when they were dislodged from their hereditary positions as helmsmen of the household by their daughter-in-law, by rejecting their stature as fatherly or motherly figures; and following in the foot-steps of his spouse, the husband also started showing them their proper places. Thereby breaking the nexus of usurers and foolish households! Thereby shooing away the perennial wretchedness they were in and I was in!

The above was true chiefly of fatherly figure. Brother, of course, objected to my writing anything true about 'his' father who, incidentally, was 'my' father, too. This inextricable knot cannot be undone by any means. This ingenious fellow, however, who himself claims to be an author and a poet of no small repute, ironically wants to see me flourish as a prolific writer, too. But not at the cost of writing anything purely true about my life or the life of my parents or relatives, for that matter, which are inextricably intertwined with my life and experiences.

I have, therefore, now decided to go ahead without taking these nay-sayers into confidence or giving them any importance.

Nevertheless, whereas my father has since been consumed by the omnipotent force called time or, so to say, has been subdued in the vortex of time, my spouse is still alive and holding forte and is as antagonistic to the core towards me as ever, albeit a bit mellowed by her state of health both physically and mentally: due in turn to the advancing age which is inescapable. Death is inescapable, too: but for that I cannot keep waiting indefinitely any longer. In the process I may also precede her!

I have found a way out of this ever haunting and ever daunting menace, that is, the obstructive presence of my spouse at least by hoodwinking her by resorting to English language as a medium insofar as she is a *dhakkan* (duffer) in respect of that *lingua franquois*. I can write anything without any fear of being caught by her, by getting read by her, in other words. There are benefits of illiteracy as well, as in my case. Illiteracy is a boon in this case: a boon for proliferation and protection of truth. And for writing truth!

What I am coming around is the fact that my spouse also has been objecting tooth and nail to my writing about herself inasmuch as her real self and her demeanour all along has been unwritable. She has torn off countless number of pages or leaves comprising my creations from my manuscripts, written of course in *Hindee* , out of rage whenever she happened to peep into those papers in her leisure time, although she seldom likes to read any *kaalaa akshar* (written, literary things). That can, in turn, be interpreted as the sign of greatness of my nascent writing efforts insofar as even un-literary person like my spouse who never ventures to read an alphabet, what to say of a word or a sentence, or even literary persons, like my father or my brother, who praise truthfulness in literary creations whole-heartedly, were obliged to browse through my rough-shod jottings. To pounce upon anything objectionable and preclude that! Because they were and are the subject matters of my writing! What else can one write about if not about one's real self and about those coming across one's trajectory of life?

If a person is the subject matter of a writing, one cannot be indifferent to that, however non-literary one might be!

People are seen commenting – especially, the writers and poets -- that there are no readers of written word these days; that the people are not interested in reading irrespective of whatever you offer. From my own experience in personal life I can say that if people themselves are made the subject matter of a writing they can in no way overlook the writing: they will have to read those writings, however explosive might be the revelation and the concomitant reaction following that.

Reaction or no reaction, it's immaterial for a writer of real worth. A true writer does not take cognizance of the amount of explosion one's writing might engender if one has stuck to his guns: to truth. He must needs to be interested only in making everyone the subject matter of one's writing so as to make them interested in reading his creations.

Next comes the question of writing for whom, that is, as a reader; for whose consumption, benefit or simply interest?

I shall write for my grandchildren who need to be taught how to ferry through the labyrinth of life, the world, the society, which is perfectly irrational, insensible and even rash, and not infrequently. My experiences of life are a reservoir of solutions to all such probable questions and labyrinths. I have been perceiving all the events – both happy and melancholy – with the eyes of a mathematician, with the aim of finding as though a unique solution to the mathematical problems. Also, to realise and accept the fact that there is no solution if that be the case eventually! To reach the realisation that there is no solution

to a certain problem is also a great achievement or a solution, so to say, in my view.

Writing for my own grandchildren – and for those of others, too – shall give me stimulation enough to remain creative and will fill me with a sense of responsibility and purpose while writing. I shan't be able to take any liberties in that instance because my own grand kids would be reading it; and any insensitive or insensible material therein might be injurious to their life-contents.

XXX

2. The Ultimate Task

Enter Protagonist

The specific task that I have ultimately to perform now in this final phase of my life is 'To Die'.

Yet there are a whole lot of living beings who would not subscribe to my suggestion of life's final rite to be 'To Die'. They would contend that dying is not the ultimate aim of life, rather, doing mundane chores, like shopping for vegetables, or pursuing feats of grave significance, like self-sacrifice for the motherland, are the tasks assigned for the remainder of life post-retirement, that is, post the period of servitude to some Govt machinery or private businessman for earning a living while traversing the length and breadth of this planet.

But I still feel that what I

think is more true or what they call 'truer'.

I have felt it palpably that everything whatsoever has been vanishing invariably in this Creation; all the living beings have been dying, too; all my relatives have already passed off; everything has changed inexorably since my childhood; not only that all have died, but also, those who are living shall die any day inescapably. My heart starts choking to think that I shall die any day likewise; I feel utter suffocation.

Oh, all this is merely a wilderness of mobile silhouettes! How unreal this all is! So unreal indeed! Entirely fictional, entirely indeed!

When I peep into the time gone by, I contemplate: lo, there were umpteen number of souls, e.g. maternal uncles, maternal grandparents, uncles, grandparents, even my own parents and siblings, who were occupying their space on the surface of this seemingly real earth! Before my eyes! Really! Or unreally? During this tenure of so many years of my bygone life-span! Presently, none of them is to be seen; albeit how material they felt at that time! How significant, as also, great! The absolute fact is that even at that juncture, they had no material significance. Anyway, none of them is existent anywhere at present. Also, those who claim themselves to

be alive and sanguine presently are bound to be dead sooner or later; there is no breach possible in that flow.

And we too shall die; my wife will die too!

I do not mind my death, for I would be gone on dying, but those who are left behind suffer so much! Oh, my wife will die too! I also begin to grieve for the wife I am constantly squabbling with. No matter how much I grieve, one day one of us has to go first, leaving the other behind! Bereaved! Even as the bereaved one has to mourn and suffer!

And there in the novel 'The Buried Giants' of Nobel Literature Laureate, *Kazuo Ishiguro* also, there is depicted almost the same theme in that a couple has turned aged; their son having already gone – gone in the murder during communal or ethnic strife or cleansing, so to say. They live and wander around aimlessly together. Their memory has gone too – Alzheimer. They however are hallucinated that their son has gone somewhere getting estranged with them, on some trifling issue. However, they saunter around together for deriving sense of safety and longevity, nonetheless, alas! the death too could have come simultaneously! Together! It didn't.

In fact *Ishiguro* has depicted death in the manner of a sailor, who avers somewhat to this effect: 'In this small boat only one passenger may fit, not two at all.' However, attached one may feel towards anybody, at the time of departure – death – one has to travel alone only!

This realisation fills me with utter sense of scare, utter ephemerality of the Creation, the meaninglessness of our existences, and at the same time, of the mindless rat race for attaining phony summits.

In the words of *Buddha,* it's all ill, suffering, misery, that I have been feeling. The world is suffering; in entirety. There is nothing in this created universe but the phenomenon of suffering and misery.

The suffering is, however, owing to attachment which, in turn, is owing to *sanskaars* -- conditioning. This creation is a wilderness of unreal images, shapes or silhouettes. Those whom we call as our own people, our relatives, our siblings, they are 'not' in reality; in absolute reality. Nowhere! All of them vanish and disappear after a gap in time. For those who seemed to be here earlier in time have all vanished inexorably. How real they felt, though at the material time! Even those who seem to be there at present shall vanish any day; how real and material they seem to be although!

We shall vanish, too, definitely. Even at the cost of

repetition, I would say, this Creation is but the ocean of suffering and misery! There is nothing in it but suffering and miseries!

By way of practice of *Vipashyanaa,* nevertheless, I know that my sorrows and sufferings are not in fact for those whom I miss on their demise, rather, the mournful feeling is due to the conditioning of my mind as such and formation of various glands in my body; that is, within me. The sensations arising within my body and mind engender the feeling of fear and scare due to my conditioning as such which *Buddha* dubbed as *Sangyaa.* Whereas the sensation – for that matter, any sensation whatsoever – is nothing but the rising and vanishing of the phenomena. If one can attain to the stage of realising that it's not fear, rather, merely the rising and ending of the phenomena, which I have construed as a matter of sorrow, the suffering will go.

Thus, our sorrows are for the attachment towards someone or something, and that is due to conditioning of our mind, that is, body as such. If one could condition them otherwise, the suffering would end; then there would be no missing of anybody on one's death or departure.

This is also an experienced fact that nobody mourns anybody forever on anybody's death. All are dying, and the survivors mourn the dead for a day or two only, and then they busy themselves in the rigmarole of life and world. The bitter reality is that if those gone by comeback getting resurrected, none alive here would like to receive them, or welcome them.

Nonetheless, this realisation fills the heart and mind with an unselfish love towards every creature on this planet. On this realisation, one starts wondering how anybody can be a stranger for anybody; all are our own only! All the kids are our own only! All! None is a stranger here, all are related to us only.

Where everybody has to die ultimately, who can be called an alien and who our own! All are wretched, all are miserable! Love everybody; love the whole of Creation! Have compassion in heart for one and all! Have infinite goodwill and best wishes for one and all! Wish welfare of everybody without exception! Don't hate anybody; don't harbour malice towards anybody! Nobody is anybody's foe! Not only the human species, but also, the other species, like fledgelings, birds, reptiles, worms, beasts or animals, all are like us only, the living beings only. They are invariably related to us, alike us only. The only difference is their body and shape, but they are just like us. We can be born as the species they are now.

But before dying, is it essential to create a record of whatever I did and feel, or so to say, suffer during all this chunk of time, small or long, that I got at my disposal, by whom I don't know?

The only temptation for creating a record of my feats what they dub as 'writing' is that only those are immortal or are known on this planet who have left something written for their progeny; others have simply vanished into thin air without leaving any trace whatsoever thereof.

Yet, in the ultimate reckoning, it is immaterial or inconsequential for those who have left here for eternity whether anybody reminisces them or not after their demise. But I think, and majority of those living here reckon, that it certainly matters for those who live presently to know or to have pre-knowledge of the course of events that may take place on this planet while treading the ever uncertain chequered board of what is called life, on which, they would have little command. Ironically, nobody can have any command over what they claim to be their 'own' life! So much possessiveness notwithstanding!

The script of life seems to have been written by someone absolutely obscure! From the eyes of actors on the stage of life, on this globe, on this planet!

It, therefore, behoves of those living presently to create trace-marks of their journey, their path on the sands of desert they happen to tread by dint of sheer chance. This they do by replacing the sand particles by spread-sheets of parchment called 'paper'. Although both are ephemeral in ultimate run. So that those wretched ones who follow them in the life's sequence may derive some solace from these traces as to the correctness or erroneousness of their foot-prints on the journey of life.

One does not live life on perfect lines, i.e. in accordance with what is desired of one by the unknown power! Yet, after creating a foul, one does realise, sooner or later, in the interiors of his corporeal mechanism what should have been the correct course of action or thought.

It is with this perspective and hindsight that I intend to record my life's journey 'as such' on the papers. Trying to be perfectly true and naked – truth can be veritable only when it is naked, nude – for the sake of posterity: my grandson and my granddaughter, to be specific and selfish, in the material sense. But the import of my writing will not be confined to only these two creatures, rather, this may be made use of by other innumerable siblings of those coming after me on this indivisible globe as a whole.

It is yet uncertain – albeit, vouchsafed by Lord *Buddha* – that I shall return in another garb here only and at some other geographical place. It is, therefore, in my self-interest as well in that these tracings of my lives by-gone shall come handy in my next attempts on the path of life on this planet in coming lives. Unless I attain '*Nirvana*' as the *Buddha* says!

To be impartial in this affair, I would like different actors of my life's drama, like, father, mother, grandfather, maternal grandparents (*Naanaa-Naanee*), wife, brother, maternal uncle (*Maamaa*), cousins etc. themselves to reminisce and narrate theirs as well as my story to my progeny. It's sort of resurrection of ancestors and contemporaries to this *yajna* of life's saga.

XXX

Table of Contents

3. The Narrative Sets Off

Enter Father

Lo, there, at work in the field, on the outskirts of our hamlet, presently, in this scorching if only pleasant sunshine is my eldest son. He is fastidious to the extent – people call it perseverance though-- that he does not mind the ferocity of weather or climate when it comes to using his physique in the agricultural fields. Especially, when it is in relation to livelihood, that is, *Rotee, Kapdaa* and *Makaan* (Food,

13

Clothing and Shelter)! He contends that even these rudimentary essentials of life are lacking in our household, that is, my household. That this is all attributable to me, my lethargy, my indolence, my aversion to industriousness or my disenchantment from any type of labour – physical, to be precise!

He is weeding out creepers, grass and undergrowth from the crop – millet – sown in this five acres of arable piece of land which, among other pieces of land, we own. Quite in the vicinity of our village! That's a privilege, a status symbol, of course! They say, only influential people can manage to own up lands in the proximity of their villages or habitats. There is an iota of truth in this conviction insofar as my forefathers had been quite influential, powerful, so to say, in their area. Quite rich! Landed gentry! And musclemen! Too. Albeit my father was the one at whom the tradition of strength of pedigree set off degenerating. The only perceptible cause for this sudden turn of fate, to me, seemed that he and his cousin had been to 'school'. Schooling: first time anybody in the family annals had done this! That was sort of experimenting with the deflection from illiteracy. Power or primacy of illiteracy heretofore had been unquestionable in the family history, even as, sort of time-tested one. It

had the effectiveness in the sense as well that no wise or literate person could dare argue or debate with our ancestors, being fully aware, without any iota of doubt, that they would not heed or comprehend anything but their own mind and their own convictions which verged on the periphery of superstitions or conventions. Superstitions that were garbed as *'shaastra-sammat'* (in accord with the *Hindoo* Gospels) traditions, deviating from which would definitely invite wrath of gods or Almighty! They were preached accordingly by their wily *Purohits, Brahmans, Pandits,* as they reverently called them.

"*Eh* Master, you do not feel ashamed or embarrassed or have any qualms of conscience about your taking bath here under the tap of this hand-pump whilst your adolescent son is exerting in the scorching heat in the field trying to weed out the poverty of your family….. He will definitely pull your family out of wretchedness you have landed them in owing to your indolent or dissipated life-style….."

Exclaiming like this is an inhabitant of our hamlet, a not-so-distant relative of ours, our cousin. He is passing by our male habitats as well as cattle pen and yard while returning from his agricultural fields, ferrying on his head the load of fodder for his cattle. I feel a strand of shame or, so to say, a slight shaking of conscience in my inner self on hearing this chastisement at the hands of my cousin. Nonetheless, I respond by keeping reticent, thinking simultaneously that this boy of mine has so far ever been a trouble creator for me; he pushes me out of my comfort zone in which I want to remain notwithstanding my impoverished condition of living. I am after all a scion of *zamindaars* (landlords) owning large tracts of land; and in our family it is considered as demeaning to make one's hands dirty by working in the agricultural fields or on machines. In our culture, living by not working or not doing anything, and simply by manipulating or exploiting poor folks, is considered 'greatness', 'elitism'. Nobody minds our family's illiteracy; we are considered all-knowing. And all-powerful as well. Even Govt service or any sort of service is looked down upon as unbecoming of our status, that's why my father never took up a salaried job. Rather, he felt contented in his short-sightedness insofar as finally, in due course, he found himself and his family in utter poverty, not very distant in future, post-colonial reign, to be precise. That is, after *'Aazaadee'* (Independence), that is, the departure of Britishers. This imminent wretchedness and impoverishment was the meaning of

Aazaadee for these and the like -- such other millions of landed gentry.

But this boy has placed me in tight spot. That rogue of a cousin of mine has passed unreasonable strictures against me; what right has he got to discredit me like this when I am enjoying my warm forenoon bath under the tap of my hand-pump! Twist in the thorny tale is that this fellow – my cousin -- would return to his fields after taking his food at home and might again create a ruckus if he passes by here again and sees me still not supporting my son in the field. I have no choice! Hobson's choice it is! I have to go join this son of a bitch in the agricultural field; and dirty my hands and holy body along with him.

XXX

4. The Saga Of Inactivity And Indolence

Enter Father

I pull off myself to the agricultural field unwillingly. I pick up a dibber and sitting alongside my son I too start uprooting the weeds and unwanted undergrowth and creepers from the millet crop. The field is strewn with spots of human nightsoil all around. It's only human excreta that stinks obnoxiously; no animal excreta stinks: cow's dung is rather a purifier! One can purify one's habitat by smearing its walls and floor with the paste of cow dung! A measure of deep chasm between the quality of innards of human beings and those of other animal species!

After a while, while exerting in the agricultural field, I feel an itching for giving vent to my inner feelings: the feelings that I harbour all along, which nobody at this hamlet is willing to appreciate. I, therefore, venture to narrate my tale of woes to my son; the son who perceives me as a deranged person, a mad man, an indolent creature, even though he has never expressly uttered those feelings to my face. But his attitude towards me betrays it all.

"My son, while weeding out or while working in the field it is advisable to indulge in some sort of fascinating tale or gossip so as to divert the mind from getting bored and from getting the body wearied. It's indeed admirable now I feel – after picking up the dibber and having started working alongside you in the field – that it is essential to weed out unwanted undergrowth from the crop. For a better harvest! Indeed, it's good, admirable! You are indeed sensible and wiser in having undertaken this task!

"Today I intend to narrate my own story. For the sake of your consumption. So that you may clear off the misconceptions and misinformation about me from your mind in that I am a lethargic and feckless person, an indolent person, a person averse to physical activity and, in turn, good for nothing."

At this volition of mine, my son, I felt, startled, as though he was ever curious to uncover the mystery of my – as per him – 'deranged' behaviour. Deranged, because he used to watch me behave – rather, misbehave – always in an unseemly manner, violent manner, uncivilized manner with his mother – and also, though slightly moderately, with his siblings, with the kids as well, whenever I happened to be in their company. My image in my son's eye of mind was that of a tyrant – a daemon, rather – with a robust stick in my beastly hands and stalking that on the feeble back of his skinny mother. Or, that of a lout who kept on throwing tantrums at the slightest excuse at the time of having food in the house. Or, someone who always was seen shouting at whomsoever came his way, especially, the youngsters who used to be innocent and came across him while busy with their innocuous plays or games. He thinks that I derive sadistic, daemonic pleasure from such insolent misdemeanours of mine.

"I was born, as you see, in a joint family which was influential, or at least it was made to be believed that way to us. Influential in those days signified powerful, authoritarian, or tyrannical, in a physical sense. My father was the same pioneer personality who had been to school with his cousin and had been rendered labour-averse as a result of his schooling. That might be the prime characteristic of English schooling!

"My mother was from a not-so-nearby village, from a family quite well-to-do. To arrange marriages in well-to-do families only was the norm of that epoch. Marrying in impoverished families, howsoever worthy or beautiful the girl or boy might be, was considered demeaning and below the standard of a worthy family. Feudalistic thinking! Engraved deep in the grooves of the grey hemispheres of the landed gentry by the wily pedants called *pandits*, that is, *purohits* of the family, the intellectual guides of their illiterate lords, demi-gods! My mother was a pretty woman endowed with profuse richness of feminine attributes. As one can vouchsafe from the anatomy and countenance of her sister, my maternal aunt who happens to be the wife of our elder paternal uncle, who is loosely related to our family too.

"My father, after finishing the schooling or, more precisely, after dropping from his education at school along with his cousin had settled at his village, this hamlet. He, used to as he was, did not do anything except sauntering around riding a mare of fine breed, donning a straw hat – of British make - that he used to put on in the school to follow suit along with colonialists. My grandfather, who was a person of quick wits, and also, a fine story-teller and a voracious conversationalist, sported a running beard and was blessed with a robust personality. He was a highly sociable person and knew when and what to do or talk to whom and when. He and his elder son were the keepers of the household and were running the only vocation, that is, farming, of which they had vast tracts. Plentiful of harvest that they reaped every season was enough to maintain a high standard and to squander, too, on profligacies: of the likes of my father.

"My grandfather did bear the profligate and indolent life of my loafing father for a year or two. Nonetheless, ultimately he ventured to offer the sane advice to my father one day when the latter was preparing to set off for a ride on his mare one fine forenoon. He proffered, *'Baaboojee!* (this he uttered in sarcasm, not in reverence, even as, my father was the only one with the appellation of *'Baaboojee'* in the whole area, not only in my village.) enough is enough! Too much of loitering around! Without doing anything! Without dispensing anything for the joint family! Whereas others are toiling from dawn till dusk through noon! Do take off these British raiment and don a peasant's apron and come down to the earth and field, to be precise, and dirty your hands now…..' *blah, blah blah*.

"This was it! As was his upbringing, my father did not utter a word in protestation. He simply dismissed his journey, took off his elegant dress, took off his aristocratic straw hat and changed into a peasant's garb - of dusky coloured loose *kurtaa* and a *dhotee* wrapped around his waist. Ever since then he was seen in those raiment only; he was never ever seen in shirt-pant or donning the hat. He was never ever seen going on sojourns with his chums of college days.

"The hat is the same hat that I put on sometimes in mirth and you keep on playing with; with so much disregard for it." I told my son.

"Oh, that hat is the piece of antique, a part of our family history, a heritage item, so important, connecting me to the British *Raaj*, I didn't ever know!" my son averred if startled, "How could one? Unless informed by someone!"

"That's why it is important to tell the tales of one's real life to the progeny so that the latter can place themselves in proper perspective while treading the course of life on this uncharted planet called Earth!" I asserted.

"So that, one does not merely take oneself for a wretched peasant, smelling the stench of nightsoil in the crops and fields!" my son exclaimed, "We are all part of a glorious history, too! Of the nation! Of our glorious past!"

XXX

5. Motherless Child Turns Mad

Enter Father

"Would you like me to tell the story of my life from the beginning or just one off anecdotes?" I interjected.

"From the beginning!" my son went on enthusiastically as if he were ever anxious to unveil the mystery of my tyrannical behaviour.

"In my babyhood I was a very robust bodied kid. Just like proverbial *Bheem* of *Mahaabhaarata* repute! I had the habit of hitting the babies of my age. Cruelly, as they say. I struck my sturdy skull against the tender skulls of others and, as a result, the babies used to cringe with pain. Still I cared two hoots for their sufferings. I was so intoxicated with my bodily prowess.

"My mother, of course, oftentimes forbade me from indulging in such *adhammik* (wanton) activities, even as, she used to preach me that every unwholesome seed of action bears unpalatable fruits of unbearable miseries. But to no consequence so far as my misdemeanour went.

"My father was a self-esteemed person if only callous by nature; he did not take care of his wife, nor did he care for us, his issues. The composition of society and families – joint families – was like that only in those days: one did not have privilege of looking after one's own issues oneself. Other family members were obliged to take due care of one's children but himself.

"Once it so happened -- we don't know how – that our father developed a rift with our mother and stopped visiting ladies' residences (*Baakhar*). You know, there are separate residences for males and females and still separate ones for the cattle. There was enough land in possession of joint family to afford such profligacies. Our mother sent repeated missives to the father for visiting her at home and to have at least his food. But my father, it seems, was a fastidious person, an arrogant person. He refused to oblige and instead opted for milking the buffaloes – which were there quite a lot of them those days in the family's possession – and continued to survive on drinking only raw buffalo milk for days together. It is not, therefore, that it is only me and your mother who indulge in domestic violence or rift, our forefathers have all along been in fight with their female folks throughout our family history! My mother even used us children as emissaries of truce between her and her husband but to no avail.

"Mother was sick at that time, or fell sick due to this tussle - I do not know - but she fell sick seriously; this is now certain when viewed in the hindsight. I being a kid of innocent age at that time did not realise the gravity of the situation. Not minding my mother's illness I kept on playing outside, beating time and playmates as well in all sorts of indulgences as usual. My mother on one such fateful day pleaded with me to go nearer her and heed her for something very crucial to be conveyed, but I was a child with little knowledge and good sense about the mysteries and abruptness of life and death. And death! That day my mother had fervently called me to go near her, even as, she looked very weak and pale, but I went past her rejoicing in my childish errands. I fled from the home preferring play. Convinced in my childish fancy that the entire scene around my life was permanent, as though fixed in some permanent frame!

"But that day, not long thereafter, I heard cries of men and women wailing, arising from my house. I could not fathom what was happening. I rushed towards my home. To my mother's care as any baby would in the face of wailing and weeping. I could never imagine that my mother could ever die, least of all, so soon and so abruptly. On entering the home, I found that my mother was lying on the ground surrounded by all family members, and also, by dozens of village folk. Mother's eyes were closed and her body inert with slight grimace on her face. She had 'died'!

"My mother was no more! For the first time I came face to face with this grave realisation. My mother was calling me to go near her. Before her death! She would be longing to embrace her youngest son for the last time. I could not understand that. My mother would not come back now. This thought started haunting me ferociously. I started crying loudly, full throat. I wept and wept and wept. For hours together. No words of solace from so many throats of family members – my elder aunt, uncles, sisters, brothers – could pacify my grief. My world had changed permanently! My child's play had been destroyed cruelly by God! In my ignorance! Had I known it, had I had a prescience of it, I would not have gone to play with children. I would have stayed back with my mother. Possibly my mother would not have died after embracing me; possibly getting life energy she would have drawn from the pleasure she would have derived from his son's embrace in that condition of melancholy and sickness.

"I wept, I lamented, I wailed: very grievously for hours together. And after a while I felt that something had cracked inside my brain, my mind, my grey matter. This I felt quite conspicuously, quite palpably, quite obviously. Thereafter, I could never be normal, I could never feel my brain under my command; it started acting arbitrarily without any control of my will power over it. As though I and my brain got disjointed."

At this point, even as, I stopped, rather paused, my son was seen sighing as if heaving a sigh of relief on the realisation that his father himself had confessed to his being deranged. So unassumingly! This filled him with assurance that it was not his father's fault to behave unseemly, rather, it was all the fallout of a chain of events in my life. How far is a man responsible for his behaviour given the fact that one's brain is deranged and is not under his control? One deserves only pity, sympathy. I contemplated that here-onwards my son would treat me sympathetically, well aware now that he was about his father's tragic tale and consequent deformity engendered in his father's brain.

It was still sometime to go before we could call it a day and leave for lunch. I, therefore, ventured to narrate another life event of mine.

"Time passes of its own!

Wounds heal too! I began to go to school, however, more irascible a child now than before! At home, at school, with companions, with family members, with all and sundry, my behaviour had become very rude and unreasonable. I broke into fits of shouting at the slightest provocation. People could not stand and fathom my tantrums. They started taking me for a deranged personality.

"One day while at school, we heard the news that '*Gaandheejee*' had been killed. Our school immediately declared holiday in mourning for the '*Mahaatmaa*'. We students, kids, were elated instead. It was off, courtesy *Mahaatmaa*, courtesy his killer -- whosoever he was! We came running back to village, shouting and chanting, '*Gaandheejee* is killed! Hurrah, *Gaandheejee* is killed!' On reaching home, when our elders including our father forbade us from chanting like that, more so, from merry-making like that, we realised that *Mahaatmaa*'s murder was not a matter of merry-making, rather, it was a moment of grieving for us alongside the countrymen. That we were duty-bound to *Mahaatmaa* for mourning on his death! In other words, it was a moment of sorrow and grief. For the entire country, which had only recently been declared free. Free from the foreign yoke, that of Britishers!

Even feeling sorry and when needs to be taught in childhood.

Incidentally, seeing my psychic predicament post my beloved mother's untimely demise my maternal uncle took me along to *Dheemaree* village, my *Nanihaal*, for giving me some semblance of solace. There, of course, in the company of my cousins – sons and daughters of my maternal uncle – I tried to calm down my mind and heart, however to little avail. There my maternal uncle admitted me to a school, as well, where I studied for a few preliminary, rather primary, classes; and had good memories of that period. Later on, for the higher grades, I shifted to my village, including the colleges at *Khurjaa* and *Ajmer*.

However, for paying back for the magnanimity shown by my maternal uncle during my calamities and for arranging for my studies during those primary years, when I became *ad hoc* teacher at *Jhaajhar* school after plucking at B. Ed. Exam I brought one of my younger cousins from *Dheemaree* to pursue his studies at my school and to board and lodge at my establishment. And that arrangement continued for a few middle and High School level grades.

When I was narrating this tale as a sequel to my mother's untimely as well as psychologically calamitous death, my son ventured to interject, "Oh! Now I can recall that uncle of ours, that one from *Dheemaree*. I was so fond of him initially to think and suppose that he was from 'our' household; and he showed lot of affection and caressing attitude towards me, too. For that matter, at that younger age all the children are shown love and affection only, and it is also true that all those gestures are sham, having no genuine substantiality therein. Nevertheless, that excessive caress and affection assumes the form of addiction or a privilege in the childish psyche of the baby insofar as the slightest deviation from that condition hurts the feelings of baby tremendously.

"In this backdrop, I have a sorry tale to narrate in that my uncle in question had slapped me the baby quite cruelly; and I can still recall that hurt and humiliation after more than half a century. It so happened that my mother asked me to go and call out for uncle for having food. I went and called the uncle in the usual childlike manner, oblivious of the worldly reactions, or so to say, the histrionics of the world of adults. My uncle was in fact dead asleep at that moment at our *Khedaa*, the males' residence. When he did not budge or did not get nudged from his *Kumbhkarnee* slumber, I unmindful of dangers associated with the world of adults went straight to his *charpoy* and started calling him putting my mouth just on his ears, *"Chaachaa! Chaachaa! Rotee Khaa Aao! Beebee bulaa rahee hai!"* (Uncle! Pray, have your food; my mother has sent for you!")

"He did not budge still. He was dead asleep, or he was just feigning to be asleep, I don't know. In my child-like zeal I repeated the act of calling him out just in his ears; and laughed in mirth, as if it was an interesting child game.

"When I repeated the feat for the third time, quick came the slap from the sleeping *Buddhaa* – my uncle – and came quite sharp and forcefully inasmuch as I felt as if my head had been made to whirl in giddiness. The five fingers of cruel uncle's hand were there imprinted on my soft chubby cheeks. I started weeping, however, to my uncle's utter embarrassment. I had been disillusioned forever as regards my uncle's affection and kindness. Immediately my baby mind decided that I would never ever forgive my uncle for that cruel and unwarned slap. And I haven't!

"Later on, when on reaching home, I complained to my mother that uncle had slapped me, she felt sympathetic towards me, but she could do nothing against the favourite cousin of her husband, however, cruelly he might have behaved."

When my son had finished

his tale, I told him that I did not know anything about that episode. Nonetheless, I explained to my son that life was full of such innumerable episodes, and he had better forget and forgive all such trivial incidents in life for the sake of mental peace in life. I also explained to him that it is exactly what the *dhamma* signifies: 'to forget and forgive!'

XXX

6. Fate Defined

Enter Father

"After finishing my schooling at the nearby town, upto Metric - that is, class 10th, I went to an Inter College, to a nearby city. And thereafter to a College, also, in the same city. Both were prestigious institutions of their time, established as those were by very glorious persons. The businessman, the *Seth*, who established the College was so influential that whenever he happened to visit *Kolkaataa* (called in those days as *Calcutta*), the Capital of East India Company, he used to be the guest of honour at the Governor General's. Once, the grapevine has it, it so happened that he went to *Calcutta* and happened to call on the Governor General who was incidentally fast asleep at that moment. The footman informed the *Seth* accordingly at which the latter commanded that the footman must go tell his master that so and so had come from so and so city. No sooner had the message been conveyed to the Governor General than the *Seth* was ushered in to the reception of the Governor General. Such was the stature and the level of influence of some Indians even in those days -- the heydays of Britishers! They were the celebrities who established such rare institutions of learning in those days."

"Not that everybody prostrated before the white, as is depicted in history books, especially, written post the euphoria of Nationalism!", exclaimed my son, to which, I nodded assertively.

"Here, let me delineate my financial woes for your consumption and better understanding. After getting me married... Oh, but I have not told you the tragic tale of my marriage to yet!

"Let me first share the tale of my wedding and woes."

"When did you get married, that is, at what age? In which standard were you at school at that time? That is."

"I was in Intermediate class or standard, studying at Inter College. In Metric, my score was quite high by the standards of those times. My father being an educated person himself, I had the benefit of his inspired guidance and, more so, his scientific temper; also, the benefit of his command of English language which was a rarity in those days.

"Even as, I was euphoric about my academic achievements and was harbouring lofty aspirations for a golden future, my elders were harbouring diagonally different dreams. As was their wont and the tradition of the society – call it backwardness or progressiveness (as they – my elders - deemed themselves to be the latter) - when I was enjoying summer vacations after 11th standard, one day I was summoned from the playground by my elders to the male residence – the *Gher*. To the exceptionally elevated male residences called the *Khedaa*.

"There I found to my amazement quite a number of respectable and aged persons assembled there. Even in my wildest dreams, notwithstanding this assemblage, did I apprehend that the assemblage gathered there was contriving to trap me by spreading the net for preying upon me. I could not suspect in my childish wisdom that they were hounds in the hide of homo-sapiens up for something in their vested interest at my career's cost.

"One of those elderly people - who was supposed to be quite close to our family circle - proffered that they all were present there to finalise my marriage proposal – to arrange a marriage for me. With your mother! Your maternal grandfather and maternal uncle were conspicuous by their presence there very much, I could now be consciously aware. And as you know, they – your maternal folks - already had one of their women-folk in our family-fold – your maternal aunt, the elder sister of your mother, that is, your elder aunt here. I being a youth suffused with high ideals and prospects, and also, belonging to an illustrious ancestry and being the scion of a father as great as mine one at that juncture, they could think of no other better proposal for their daughter than me. And age – minor or innocent – was no criterion worth consideration in those days. I was at that time only 18! You can just imagine! What would have been my condition at receiving this heart-rending proposal! I reacted with a loud outburst, 'Never! Not at all!'

"Then started cajoling. By elders. All sorts of commutations and permutations! But I kept stuck to my guns. I could not sacrifice my ambitions - of completing higher studies - at any rate. When ultimately nothing worked..."

"Did your father not come to your rescue at such a crucial moment? He was educated and was consequently supposed to be a rational and modern persona, also endowed with scientific temper as he was, as you have already told and as we ourselves had also found him so during our interactions with him during his lifetime?" interposed my son with amazement and some amount of vexation.

"Oh no! Not at all! He remained absolutely indifferent as though it was a no-brainer for him. He never used to behave as our father: he never showed any reaction or betrayed any emotions on facing us children. Even after our mother's death, when we were left mere wretches, mere orphans! At the mercy of our aunts and uncles! Yes, of course, his elder brother, *Netaajee,* was quite a considerate and kind human being, even as, he was quite pragmatic. He used to take ample care of us children. Like a *de-facto* father! Here, I would like to add that there was nothing unusual about it; this was the norm, the general trend of the times, of the social set-up; other family members used to own up the issues of their siblings, to the exclusion of their parents. Maybe with a view to instilling a sense of belonging in the joint family.

"Finally, when I frustrated all their efforts at cajoling me into their net for their own merry-making on the pretext of my marriage ceremony, even at my career's cost, I set off moving away from there muttering and gibbering something odd. At that point, the same elderly person who feigned to be our so-called well-wisher (he had shown profuse pity, empathy and sympathy post-demise of our mother and genuinely had nothing ill towards us) caught hold of me and unsuspectingly put his skullcap on my feet entreating, 'Our prestige is in your hands, beloved son; we have already promised to them your hand; we do not intend any harm to you, rest assured, how can we? Please consent to what we say!... For salvaging our prestige, for keeping our word!'

"And thus there was no way out! Of this net! Of this sentimental blackmail. Of these fetters of social affiliation!", sighed my son grievously adding, 'And they fulfilled their fraudulent and orthodox dreams at the cost of your feelings, aspirations and career! And life! Very sad!.... You should have still denied.' He concluded.

"Now in the hindsight it can be inferred like that safely, but in the heat of moment and especially in the then prevailing social mores, it was not possible for an eighteen year old lad, who had yet not finished his schooling, to revolt against deep-rooted social superstitions and orthodoxies, more so, against the emotional blackmail! At this moment, of course, I feel that the right and judicious decision would have been to stick to my guns and to refuse nonetheless. I would advise you to adopt that course of action, rather, if such a situation presents itself to you."

"And we are here in this agricultural field weeding the undergrowth to recite, *Hoi hai soi jo Raam rachi raakhaa!* (Gods will be done!)" sighed my son and I sighed, too, 'Yes! That's how people ultimately start having faith in the fate.'.

"Obviously, the fate is nothing but the surrendering to vicious cycle of circumstances created by social orthodoxies and superstitions and emotional blackmailing by vested interests or ignorant elders disguised as our well-wishers!", concluded my clever son.

XXX

7. *Presentiments*

Enter Naanaajee *(Maternal Grandfather)*

Almost moribund, lanky bodied, I now feel like dying as soon as possible. This inevitable chore of life's journey must now get accomplished without any further awaiting. I have been a successful land-holder, a successful house-holder and a respectable personage of my area. Most of my feats in this life-span have been perfectly executed, and also, to my satisfaction; yet I have a few failures of judgement to my account which I lament no end!

Weather at the moment, incidentally, is salubrious, warm, soothing to my aging body. There can be no better medication for the corporeal body of an old man than the profuse usage of sunshine. My youngest daughter could not be settled well; she has all along been living a wretched existence post her wedding. Ironically, she was my most favourite and dearest child and I was fond of her. How I craved to settle her in a care-free life when she was just a baby! She had never known a frustration or sorrow in her childhood while staying at ours. How pretty were her looks when she was just a toddler! Then an adolescent! Then a youthful blonde! And presently, what she is! An emaciated old lady! A skinny soul! Shorn of all womanly features! She looks older than I, with wrinkles all over her face and neckline! Courtesy of her good for nothing, indolent, dissipated and wretched husband! Insolent as well!

That turned out to be my gravest mistake, a blunder rather, to have solemnized marriage of my sweetest daughter with that loafer. It was in fact owing to the astuteness of my elder son-in-law, the husband of my middle daughter, who had proposed his cousin, the motherless soul, as a worthy groom for my youngest daughter when she was barely 18 or so. This one of my sons-in-law has proved to be a conceited person, sort of self-centred person, I must admit. He is actually a scion of landlords' family, son of an influential father, with the result that he has got an abnormally inflated ego. Without substance, that is! He does not even mind usurping the hard earned money of his close relatives. For instance, once, he had usurped quite a sum of my younger son's money on the pretext of borrowing on the occasion of wedding of former's daughter when my son had gone to attend the function in question to his place of marriage. My son-in-law had asked my son mirthfully to help him monetarily on that occasion and my son, unassuming and simple-hearted as he is, offered whatever he had in his pocket -- not a small sum of Rs. Ten Thousand, quite a big sum by the standards of those times -- in fond anticipation that the same would be returned on solemnising the marriage ceremony. But that was not to happen, never to happen. Even today, after so many decades, there is no mention of returning that huge sum of money which would reckon in lacs at present. That cheating resulted in souring of relations between the two close relatives, i.e.; my son and his brother-in-law.

Anyway, that is another story. That is no story anymore; that tale has remained without an ending. Time sweeps all the tales off to the trash-bin!

At the instance of my son-in-law and his father, my relatives, that is, I had solemnised marriage of my blossoming daughter with her husband who has presently, in perspective, proved to be a non-entity, to put it figuratively. An anti-climax, so to say, of my fancies for my daughter's married life.

Nonetheless, the son of my daughter is a promising prodigy. He is pursuing his studies by putting up with my younger son, the same simpleton one. In a sense, this also does tantamount to a fraud on my son's earnings. By yet another son-in-law, that is, the husband of another daughter, the youngest one. I do not know how my daughter's son feels in these straitened circumstances of stay at a relative's abode and mercy, but I am sure, my son has a big heart to have accommodated his sister's son in his house so as to facilitate the latter to pursue his higher studies. God will certainly reward my son! And my daughter's son, too!

Let me come to the point. Often on days off or on Sundays, the son of my youngest daughter happens to visit our hamlet along with his maternal uncle, my son, and he is incidentally here at present. My life-span is about to expire definitely as well as shortly. I may not be there in existence to exhort him next time. I have something obscure in my bosom to give vent to. That is, I would like to plead with her son – my daughter's son -- he is her eldest son -- something that

I have been longing to give vent to all my life. It is with this intent that I have sent for him.

And lo, he is coming.

He is here.

"*Baabaajee, namastey!*", he offers his obeisance to me.

"Be happy! Sit down." I beckon to him to be seated beside me. "Let me finish administering medicine to my eyes. This medicine was concocted and given me by *Vaidjee* of *Jaabil* village. *Jaabil* is actually a distorted version of the word '*Jaabaali*'; *Jaabaali* was a great sage of olden days."

"*Jaabaali* is the same sage who was a *Paramarshi* (an enlightened person) and who came across *Raama* during the latter's exile in the forest and offered solace to the latter when he was lamenting his unjust exile by his father and step-mother. *Jaabaali* had offered *Raama* the sane advice that in this visible world nothing has any substance, significance or sanctity at all; that even relations are sham; nobody belongs to anybody in real terms. On this fabricated stage of world or society, one should take care of one's mundane interests by dint of clever and fuller use of one's talents, both mental and physical. In other words, the sage counselled that *Raama* ought to revolt and wage a war against his father and not innocently or gullibly to obey his father's command, even as, the

subjects of his father's reign were supporting *Raama*." The son of my daughter interjected; he is in fact a very voracious reader, particularly, of classics and history.

I got curious, "How did *Raama* react to this piece of advice from *parmarshi Jaabaali*?"

"*Raama* got annoyed and infuriated, conditioned as his mind was by a particular cult of blind subjugation to one's elders' commands. However, when *Raama* got infuriated and set off upbraiding the enlightened sage, *Vashishtha, Rama's* preceptor, intervened and revealed to *Raama* the fact of *Jaabaali's* stature of an enlightened one, adding further that whatever the most revered *Jaabaali* had averred was the absolute truth, an unadulterated truth, and that the enlightened ones can't tell anything but truth, however, bitter and blasphemous that might seem to *Raama's* conditioned and specifically cultured mind."

In the meantime, I had finished applying medicine to my eyes and started off on my commission.

"Dear son! I have summoned you on special purpose."

"What purpose, *Baabaajee*? I have been only here most of my life's time-span. You have always got umpteen number of opportunities to command me." He submitted with a start.

"Yes, that's true, but I was not about to die heretofore so soon. Henceforth, I am about to die. I shall exist hardly for a year."

At this queer reply, he preferred to keep mum. Possibly, because mention of death is a taboo in our society. Living is the only thing worth mentioning. Death is not worth mentioning in mutual or social conversations.

"I have called you to tell you that I shall die soon. For that I ask you to come to me with paper and pen and then I shall dictate to you the list of persons who should be invited to my *Terahvin* (feast after 13 days of death to propitiate gods – and cunning *pandits*, to be precise). My particular request to you is that after my death and after finishing your studies you will get some job – good or bad, nobody can foresee -- but job you will certainly get. My request to you is that after settling in a job you ought not to ignore or forsake my daughter, your mother. You should take proper care of hers. Throughout her life she has been forced to live the life of a wretched person in abject penury, devoid of even two morsels of food, what to speak of clothes and habitat. She didn't get any happiness in her married life. She even used to be thrashed at her husband's inebriated hands. Her husband squandered even the last piece of whatever was called an inheritance in the household. She didn't even have wood fuel for cooking *rotees*, not even food, bare *rotees* and salt. Not to speak of clothing to cover the naked body, to protect one's shame, nor even the sandals, footwear to protect her bare feet. Choice of her husband was a great mistake on my part. That was my gravest failing, for which I shall never forgive myself and I shall die a dejected father for this guilt in my heart. My soul will never rest in peace. The only consolation for me now left seems to be begging before you to take care of my daughter, your wretched mother, when you stand on your own two feet. And please do not subject her to any further sorrow and misery." I added with tears flooding my old dimming eyes.

He felt somewhat embarrassed. He, in turn, exclaimed as if feeling hurt, as if he could not even imagine of hurting his mother, "Why should I hurt my mother and give more distress to her? Living as I do is meant for her sake only. She has always been so dear to me...." He could not add any further, choked as his throat got.

I felt a burden lifted off my chest.

XXX

Enter Naanaajee *(Maternal Grandfather)*

My daughter's son came to me with a notebook and a pen in his hand. At that time, I was seated on my *chaarpoi* (cot woven with cords) in the soothing shade of *Neem* tree in this salubrious October season.

"Write on top in bold letters: 'The list of persons to be invited for *Terahvin* ceremony of *Naanaajee*'. You have to keep this list securely and make it available to my sons when I am gone."

"Quite appalling, *Baabaajee!* Why are you up to such bizarre thinking as preparing the list of the would be invitees for your death-ceremony: the feast on death? Nobody usually does this!" He sighed with consternation, even as, he wrote what I had commanded. He smiled wryly.

"It's essential. Actually, while inviting people generally some important acquaintances are omitted by mistake, even if not on purpose. It makes sense to get prepared a list in advance so as to avoid such eventualities which later on may leave scope for regrets."

Thereafter, I dictated the entire list stretching my waning memory. As it happened, many a name were forgotten which had to be added later on when it clicked that they were not added. Then he realised that I was correct in my conviction that many names are omitted if the list is prepared in the nick of the hour and in a hurry.

"*Baabaajee*, instead of throwing feast for whole lot of acquaintances, it is more sensible to donate the body to a hospital for research work in the modern circumstances. Not only it is a more sensible step, it is in accord with the norms of *Dharma* (the Nature's Laws) in that the donation of one's body is a great donation (*Daana).* In material terms as well, it is better not to expend money on funeral and other rites including throwing of treat to all and sundry after thirteen days of death of one's beloved." He proffered, "It is plainly ridiculous and irrational."

"Nonetheless, this is a time-tested tradition. Through these rites and variegated activities (*karmkaandas*), actually what happens is that the bereaved family's attention is diverted from the lamentations and ruminations on the departed soul. Everybody knows, there is no absolute meaning in such activities (*shaastric karmkaandas*) except that these are psychological tricks to divert attention of the bereaved family to meaningless errands in the consummation of which the surviving heirs and relatives forget about the deceased person. *Shaastric* injunctions, if at all, imply relevance and meaningfulness in that sense." I clarified to him, adding, "What you are thinking is also not off the mark.

What *Shaastras* prescribe is purposeful, too, if viewed in proper perspective. Only what is obvious is not always significant, what is warranted from those activities is equally significant. Feast on death *(Terahvin)* implicitly serves the purpose of alleviating the pain and depression caused by death to the family apart from serving the purpose of conveying the message of death of that specific person to all and sundry, also, affording the fact of death sort of permanency in the memory of the community, by associating it with this indelible feat of all-pervasive treat of feast."

Whether he was convinced or not I do not know, but I overheard him conveying this news to my son and my grandsons, his playmates, after we were done with our job. He briefed them that I, being a senile person, was indulging in queer activities like that of preparing the list of invitees for my death ceremony. To this, my sons and grandsons were overheard reacting with the exclamations like, 'Oh, great! He has such a great faith in you. He chose you for this crucial task! Keep this list unto you as he has desired."

Despite that he handed over the list to my younger son with whom he was staying and pursuing his higher studies. And, in turn, my son put the list in my almirah only in which all other confidential papers pertaining to our family wealth and sundry affairs were ensconced.

XXX

Table of Contents

9. Too Great To Be Omitted

Enter Protagonist

And the insistence of *Naanaajee* on preparing the list of invitees for the feast on his death immediately reminded me of an anecdote told to me by my grandfather.

In the nearby village to ours once there was to be held a big feast. While preparing the list of invitees for the same, when it came to our village, the persons responsible for dictating the names to the scribe of the list, however, omitted the name of the most prominent person of our village, i.e. our great grandfather. The list of invitees was sent to our village observing due process and with full regards and the person who brought the list actually ensured that the list was handed to the same prominent person – our great grandfather -- only because he was the most influential person of our village at that time.

On receiving the list, out of curiosity, the recipient perused the list and found his name missing – neither in the beginning, nor at the end was his name to be found in the list. He felt a bit bemused yet didn't bring this fact – this omission --to the notice of the bearer of the letter. The bearer entreated our great grandfather to ensure that everybody from the village made it convenient to partake of the feast on the appointed date and the great grandpa assured, too, vigorously.

On the appointed date, the great grandfather accompanied by whole lot of villagers from our village made entry into the hosting hamlet. The hosts were very glad to see the great grandpa at their function – even as, it was a feast on the death of someone old from their family.

After initial exchange of pleasantries, the hosts requested the prominent guest to come forward and partake of the feast, to which, the latter responded by beckoning other villagers to partake of the feast. In one or two sittings all the villagers from our village had had their turns but great grandfather had not yet had his turn.

Then the hosts pleaded with him to himself come forward. Presently, the great grandfather dropped a bomb-shell when he apprised them that he could not partake of the feast because he was NOT invited. To this the hosts feeling bad and embarrassed responded with 'How it is possible, *Baabaajee*! Come on please! Do not play pranks, enough of it!'

But the grand old man appeared grave in his conviction and repose. He asserted that he indeed was not invited even though he had

come to accompany his villagers so that the mood of the occasion was not vitiated.

There ensued a commotion all round – how come it is possible! Not to include *Baabaa*'s name in the invitees whereas everybody else's name was there in the list!

Baabaa then unwrapped the parchment before them on which the list was scribbled and to the embarrassment of one and all, from top to bottom; the name of *Baabaa* was missing from the list.

Now what to do? How to undo this blunder? It was an inexorable shame. There were no words to seek forgiveness of *Baabaa*. Utter embarrassment permeated the atmosphere all around!

But *Baabaa* was a man of society and a seasoned one at that. It was he only who could solve this tangle, none else *a la Bheeshma Pitaamaha* of *Mahaabhaarata* repute.

He trivialised the issue and laughed off the mistake and ventured to sit on the jute straps spread on the floor for the function proclaiming, "I knew it's not intentional, it's an omission; it's owing to over importance being given to someone, too much to remember to even include his name in the invitees. Everybody might have thought that so and so is so prominent that his name would have been included already and everybody was concerned about inclusion of lesser mortals. Never mind! Come on!"

XXX

10. Karma–Danda *(Fallout Of Misdeeds)*

Enter Mother

"I am older than your father." I disclosed to my son one day when my husband fell sick. My husband has quite often been falling sick throughout his lifetime, "He will die before I die nonetheless. He is so weak-minded. I shall survive him in spite of his being younger than me, by almost two years."

"Oh no, it can't be," started my son quite amazed at this revelation, "How can a wife be older than a husband!" My son couldn't even dream of such an eventuality, such an aberration.

"Actually, unless children are educated about such matters, they continue to harbour such notions as this one: that the female partner ought to be somewhat younger than her husband. For better control over her physique and carnal demands. But this obviously sensible rule is not always observed in practice. As did in my case.

"I was quite lovely, smart, healthy, attractive, glamorous and endowed with profuse sensual as well as carnal assets. Youngest daughter of my parents as I was, I was a pampered child all along, arguably the dearest one to my parents, and also, to my brothers and sisters. The conspicuous outcome of this sort of pampered upbringing was that I was very bold, very frank and very humorous, having a ready wit and very high sense of humour. I had the gall to make fun of or play pranks on whoever one might be. Owing to this particular trait of mine I was quite often used as a tool for poking fun at the guests on the occasion of family functions whenever they happened to visit our hamlet, even as, it added to their honour and gave me pleasure – a sadistic one at that. My arrogance this way might be pretty unbearable, naturally, in corroboration of which, I not infrequently did swear at my playmates pronouncing in conspicuous terms that I 'was the daughter of so and so – my father', as if the uttering of name of my father was a warning enough to scare all and sundry. To scare the other village folk! And why not? My father was the wealthiest land-holder of the hamlet, also in the area, having quite an influence over the village folk. This situation had afforded me the self-proclaimed stature of a judge in petty disputes of children and the poor folks of the hamlet. I threw my weight around on such occasions and, in turn, might have been inviting curses of those who felt weighed down or discriminated against in the shoddy process or who might have felt deceived or cheated because of my irrational and rash denouements. Nonetheless they could not throw their tantrums before me, nor could they express their resentment before me.

"Even though unintentional, the accumulation of those unspoken curses seems to have been my undoing of fate and fortune in the later life, my married life, for that matter. Now I realise, in hindsight, but it is too late now! Alas, I could have another chance at reliving my childhood! But the drama of life has no room for replay!"

My son looked morosely at my prognosis of my prevailing wretched condition at present.

"Your father has never given me any comfort in my married life. He could not arrange even the basic necessaries of existence, that is, *Rotee, Kapdaa aur Makaan* (Food, Clothing and Habitat). Despite being a Bachelor of Arts by education! The lone B.A. of his time in the entire area! He was a scion of rich landed ancestry. He owned quite a large swathe of arable land. He inherited quite a wealth in the form of gold, silver and jewellery. He had wealthy and resourceful relatives, influential relatives. Still, he could not afford *Rotee, Kapdaa aur Makaan* for himself, nor for his five surviving children and skinny as well as lanky wife. This is a

testimony to his inferior quality of manly attributes. Neither his ancestry, neither his pedigree, neither his landed property, neither his inheritance, neither his wealthy relationships, nor his being an exclusive B.A. of his time by education came to any avail. He was the son of an only literate person – English literate one – in the area and the son of a very respectable father who happened to be having links with the who's who in the administration at various levels! He turned out to be a sham persona. Inferior to even an illiterate, invalid, handicapped and wretched person!

"My wedding was conceived initially with another youth of this village, that another rich person of your village, that wealthy landowner!" I sighed while exclaiming this and felt a sweet pain in my belly. "My fate brought me to this good for nothing lineage! Had I been married to that initial youth, I would have been living like a queen today: quite healthy, wealthy and carefree! With lots of prestige and dominance in society and the village! Today, in spite of there being every type of advantage for me in the beginning of my life's journey, nothing is left with me. I am shorn of everything! Owing to this indolent husband of mine! He gave me no comfort in life!"

"Mother, do tell us about your marriage, how it turned out to be solemnised. With our father. He does not seem to be at all a matching groom for you; now in hindsight it is quite obvious and has been proved too without any doubt. How your astute parents, who were otherwise quite sensible and pragmatic persons, could have made such a grave mistake of judgement? In wedding you, their dearest piece of heart in such a family? Of indolent and incapable people?" asked my son, as though to afford a whit of solace to my grieving and aching soul. Or, as though to feel himself some soothing sensation of coolness in the sweltering weather of summer season. Narratives of marriage and love affairs have ever been the most intriguing episodes and of utmost interest for everybody – be they children, the youth, the aged. Furthermore, such narratives catapult people mentally to the domain of time in the reverse order. It's like peeking virtually into the past. Past can be resurrected by means of vivid and picturesque narratives about our lifetimes.

XXX

11. Rendezvous As Related Ones

Enter Mother

"Now that your father is on deathbed, I don't know whether it would be becoming of me to recount the events of my life, and particularly, of my marriage ceremony. And also for you, his progeny, to listen to such tales implying mental merriment. He is suffering from cancer. At the last stage! For last four months he has not had a morsel of food or a drop of liquid including water. Nothing at all! His voice is chocking and becoming fainter by the day as a result of constriction of his vocal chord, the choking of his throat. He has throat cancer.

"And, I can see with my penetrating and pure and old eyes, without any malice towards him that his body, particularly, countenance and face have metamorphosed into that of a phantom, an apparition presently. He looks exactly like a spectre, a phantom, a fiend! Exactly such are the portraits of phantoms printed in the horror story books you read! I sometimes have been contemplating if he was *de facto* a phantom in the hide of a human who, after perpetrating all sorts of sins and tyranny on us all, has finally reached his day of denouement. He did not do his duty of even providing *Rotee, Kapdaa aur Makaan* to his wife and children as though on purpose, by design, so to say. A phantom's soul as he had, his *karma* has ultimately caught up with him. Nature has denied him food, even liquid and now even air at the last stage. He committed sins using exactly these organs: that have been choked; nature has punished him exactly through these organs by developing cancer in them. It's Nature whose judgement is unerring, unblemished and final!

"You remember, how diabolical he has been throughout his youth and adulthood in behaving with us: very much a tyrant ! He never let our lives in peace! What the devil of a husband and a male he used to be?"

"But Mom, you are not telling us the marriage story of our father; instead, you are recounting what we all know already. He is on deathbed! In his true form – a fiend. Not having had any intake of food and liquid for last four months, now not even able to utter a word, and even unable to breathe! *Karm-Dand! Katataa Nahin Hai Kintu Vajra Se Bhee Karma Toh!* (The fallout of one's actions cannot be undone even with the help of *Indra's Vajra*). One ought to be very careful about one's actions (*kammanto*), thoughts (*sankappo*) and even speech (*vaachaa*). So as to die in peace! So as to die without suffering such infernal miseries!", my son philosophised.

"During his summer vacations, one year your father had accompanied our elder sister, who is also the wife of his elder brother, to our hamlet. He was a school going lad at that time, with quite a rotund physique and with attractive

features, enough to entice any girl of the young age. It's quite natural, nothing worth hiding in it! Whenever two genders come by, there is an unintentional reaction of attraction and sensation in the carnal bodies on both the sides. I and my friends were naturally enticed by your father during the duration of that sojourn. He stayed at ours for about a month. At that time, there was no such prospect, not even germination of a thought to the effect that he would be my husband in due course. The idea might have been there in the minds of my sister and his husband though. And that may as well be the reason behind my sister taking your father along to our village during the latter's summer vacations that year.

"He was an innocent and ingenuous lad. Showing no emotions or sentiments as regards carnal feelings towards feminine folks! He was neither hesitant to talk frankly while interacting with female folks! Because in his mind he was treating us as strangers, not his would be life partners! The problem does start only when one is given the input that the other party is likely to become one's spouse in near future: then both sides become self-conscious, feeling shy, uncomfortable and disbalanced. They develop shyness and hesitancy while coming together; they start blushing in company of each another. That is the sure sign of love affair germinating: when a lad and a lass do feel embarrassed while interacting with each other!

"One such instance of providential presentiment that took place during that visit, I may narrate anyway. We all the children were playing some game verging on sort of gambling. In that game, my party was vanquished whilst the side of your father had incidentally won. The kids started pulling me up chanting that I was defeated so I owed your father a ride: that was innocent way of paying reparations of defeat to the victors. I felt let down. Then your father handled the situation astutely by remarking, 'She but is from our own *ghar* (household), therefore, no question of paying rent by riding her back. We are from the same household'. His utterance was spontaneous and innocent. But by connotation, the uttering implied that 'she is our wife, so my rent is her property'. Taking this perverse meaning, the children started making fun and laughing loudly, playing pranks, which he could but fathom quite belatedly. So innocent was he at that time!"

"How a simpleton can metamorphose into a daemon in the course of time traversing the trajectory of social life!", my son lamented, "The same lad became your husband, just coming true of your fond expectations! How wrong are our childish perceptions! Our perceptions about the prospects of lads and lasses in our and their adolescence and youth!"

"Thereafter, I do not recollect, he ever visited our hamlet before my marriage. That seemed to be a precursor to the coming events and the turning point for the worse in my fortunes in future. Even if I had an unconscious liking for him or a longing for becoming his wife at that time of summer interaction, the fire was whetted by the later developments when my sister, whenever she happened to visit our village in summer vacations of his children along with his husband – your elder uncle -- used to narrate your father's feats in the field of academics   – somewhat exaggerating, as was the wont of the entire clan at that time. They were in the habit of making a mountain of the molehill! It seemed at that time that had I been successful in getting married to him, I would be the happiest and merriest bride in the community. There was no reason for doubting this fantastical future given all the right things in place as regards my ancestry and wealth as well as his ancestry and wealth, with the added icing on the cake on his side in the shape of his exclusive higher education. So-called!"

XXX

12. Unashamedly Selling Family Jewels

Enter Father

"Thus was my fate sealed." I concluded the precursor to my child marriage through emotional blackmailing by the family elders and supposedly well-wishers – to which an adolescent is simply susceptible -- the family elders being totally insensitive to my future and career and family life. I had got deranged already by crying and lamenting excessively in the aftermath of my mother's sudden and untimely death; and now this mishap of untimely marriage – premature marriage -- turned me doubly deranged; I turned paranoid.

My son while continuing his weeding pursuit spurred me on to share the finer details of the wedding, his father's wedding, "But you had got sumptuous dowry from your in-laws as our mother claims quite often!"

"Mother often rues peevishly that her father had given hard cash of Rs.1000/- in gilt coins apart from all other adjuncts like jewellery and utensils etc." My son added zealously as if to uncover the mystery of that hidden treasure. No doubt the sum of one thousand rupees in gilt coins those days was a whopping as well as eye popping amount! In present day terms that would amount to about ten lac rupees. I had therefore to narrate the nuances of family affairs to the son. In the process of this story-telling, of course, we had forgotten that we were working in the agricultural field under the sunshine which is nothing short of extreme torture, even as, we were perspiring profusely owing to rainy season and resultant humidity obtaining in the atmosphere.

"After getting fettered by emotional chains of the family elders I had to get married and married I got soon thereafter. No doubt the in-laws gave dowry, gifts and jewellery to their and our full expectations. I, in turn, was feeling comfort of thought that I should get at least the money if I was getting a huge liability in the shape of a wife; and that the money would be helpful in pursuing my further studies which were my prime concern those days, not the marriage.

"The matter of fact is that our elder uncle, *Netaajee,* grabbed the entire bounty and I personally didn't get even a pie from that huge sum. I could get only a paltry sum which was collected during the *Teekaa* ceremony. I thought I would get the remaining sum at a later date when the dust of wedding hustle-bustle would settle down, but it was not to happen. *Netaajee* was clever in money matters to the extent that he did not reckon the interference of ethics in these matters: whoever possesses the money it belongs to one, he believed in this earthly prudence. Furthermore, he had two or three daughters of marriageable age, yet to be married and that required huge sums of money for dowry. My marriage was *de facto* a trade-off between such liabilities and my selling off in the marriage market without regard to my sentiments, psyche or the career.

"I was an adolescent of 18 years and I had a young woman now as my wife whose entire liability shifted from her father's side to me. And here were my family members who were behaving as if they had no concern for this new entrant, this new woman: that was my responsibility now, however I managed or mismanaged. There was no mention of one thousand rupees. Your *Naanaajee* is reported to have spent three thousand rupees on your mother's marriage in all. A huge wastage by the standards of those days!

"The sense of well-being that was engendered with the solemnisation of my marriage did get extinguished within no time: the utensils, gifts etc. were disposed of in the shape of giveaways during the marriages of other family girls; money as well might have been expended. Nobody was even bothered about our food, clothing and shelter after having married us teenagers: me and my wife, your mother!

"I had passed intermediate standard in 'second grade' and had to take admission in undergraduate classes at College in nearby small city, which was the only college available in the whole area. Admission required money and money it was which I didn't have (despite the impression having gone in the society that I had got a sumptuous dowry from my in-laws and that my in-laws were quite wealthy). Yet the reality was just the opposite, I was a wretch after my marriage; earlier when I was a bachelor, I was considered a part of the joint family and all my needs and demands were met religiously by my family elders. Now, no sooner had I got a woman than I was sort of segregated from the main stream of that joint set-up and was supposed to fend for myself, and also, for my wife: unguarded, unsupported. This was the irony of marriage and the reality of mirage or wealthiness!

"I was not at all interested in your mother, however, pretty and charming she might look. Your birth took place five years after my marriage.

"I was interested in my education and in my career only. Nobody in the family circle came to my rescue to advance that."

"Not even your father?" interjected my son, apparently amazed at the turn of events in my life.

"My father was a passive character; he did not own up any responsibility, nor did he lay claim to any property or money of the family. He was least concerned where my dowry money of one thousand rupees had gone or who had usurped that huge sum. Nor did he have any wherewithal to help me with my admission or tuition fees."

"Queer! It sounds quite bizarre, an irresponsible father, an ineligible father, begetter of issues without owning up any responsibility for their upbringing and career's advancement!" sighed the son.

"Our father was indifferent to family affairs or to the sentiments of his children; rather our elder uncle – *Netaajee* -- was sensible and considerate, he took care of us children like an elder must."

Somehow I took admission in BA in the prestigious College at the nearby small city, leveraging the gift money that I had got during marriage. Also, in case of further need for meeting the expenses related thereto I took the gold jewellery of your mother including your baby bangles and sold them off to a goldsmith at the town or city whatever you may call it. For that purpose, the jewellery was to be smelted and I had to sit there continuously for 5 to 6 hours. Then I got hefty sum of money and I was

flush with funds in the exchange.

"But your maths has never been strong! It was a gory exchange! Full of ill-will and lack of sentiments towards the feelings of others like your wife and your baby!" interjected my son peevishly, implying I don't know what.

"I unflinchingly squatted at the jeweller's shop and saw the jewellery getting melted and converted into glittering golden liquid. I didn't even budge for urinating. When the money came into my hands I was so thrilled. As if all my monetary problems had been put to rest for good."

"Money acquired by selling family gold or proverbial 'family silver' never helps; it only brings the end! At an accelerated pace!" sighed my son adding, "and that is quite obvious in your case. You are a pauper still. After decades thereafter! It's like earning money by selling one's body – by doing sex – alike prostitutes, who never prosper and never command respect from society and anybody, even from those who use their bodies for satiating their carnal lust!"

"I cleared all my liabilities, bought me fabulous dresses and for the rest I bought a buffalo: for fetching milk for my family and son, that is, you. When I bought the milch buffalo, my family elders were taken by surprise. They wondered where I had got the money from, for all this apparent profligacy.

"They could not suspect that I could be as foolish and reckless as to have sold even the bangles of my baby son for whom his *Naanaa-Naanee* had gifted those four lovely bangles. I convinced my wife that once I got through all the rigmarole of education and exams I would purchase ample number of bangles for her and my kids.

"That was never to happen, as my son had said, my arithmetic was very poor. The ill-gotten liquidity soon vanished and I found myself again in the grip of penury. I now sold off the buffalo too, even as, there was no one to fetch it the fodder and to take care of it. A cattle cannot survive without fodder and water! I could not permit the family ladies to venture out of house to fetch the fodder from the fields and take care of the poor cattle. That was the norm of our feudal set-up. And me? No question! I was a literate person! Only unlettered and unschooled souls are supposed to work!"

XXX

13. Wielding Sticks On Wife's Back

Enter Mother

"When I reached my in-laws' village home, as against my fancies that the house would be a splendid place, or palace, as was given me the impression, I found it a not very spacious complex in which multiple families stayed together; the atmosphere therefore therein was claustrophobic, suffocating, whereas at my father's it was an atmosphere of fresh air, greenery and freedom, even pleasure. Here, there was no question of pleasure; the atmosphere was always tyrannical.

"Most of all, the husband was a daemon incarnate, a deranged person. My in-laws didn't have any intrinsic wealth to be true. They revelled in the new found wealth through my wedding. And the first shock came when your father asked me to part with my jewellery on the pretext of meeting his expenses on education. He passed his graduation by selling my jewellery, showing no sentiments or qualms of conscience.

"Then came the question of his pursuing B Ed, the exam to qualify for entitling one to be a teacher in a local school. He did not have any other source of income other than my jewellery and the money I got as parting gifts from my parents whenever I happened to visit them – and those visits were quite frequent. My husband always waited with bated breath for my return, not because his family and wife were back, but because I would be bringing some cash for him to splurge on his dissipated life, intoxicants and his indolence.

"Since my jewellery was all consumed in due course, now for pursuing his B Ed he demanded the four lovely golden bangles that my father had gifted to you as a baby on your birth. Those were pretty things. I first resisted, more so, because of their emotional value and their link to my son, who was not aware of anything yet; and his bangles were being frittered away by his profligate and dissipated father unsentimentally. My husband lacked emotional quotient as though with the wailing for his mother he had wasted all his tears and sentiments as well. He behaved as a drunkard, as an intoxicated person always; his eyebrows were always warped and wrinkled.

When I did not budge he took a stick and started beating me on my back: he was a beast in human shape. He had been indoctrinated by his family elders in great classic poet *Tulseedaas's chaupaaee*:

Dhol ganwaar shoodra pashu naaree!
Ye sab taadan ke adhikaaree!

That was the totalitarian as well as feudal mindset that was working behind such misdemeanour. I had no option but to give away the bangles. Your father took them unabashedly and gleefully like a daemon would, catching his prey after preying upon it. He was a shameless fellow. I wailed for long thereafter. The joint family structure was such that nobody cared for anybody else but oneself. There was no meddling even in the tussles and beatings of husband and wife. It was their internal matter: of husband and wife; rather the family elders, particularly, women got a perverse pleasure in watching their young male members wielding sticks on the backs of their young spouses. This was the norm: to keep womenfolk under yoke and subjugation of male members."

XXX

Enter Mother

"During his B Ed study at *Ganj Dundwaara*, I was mostly staying at my parent's with my son. *Ganj Dundwaara* had become a buzzword those days in my parental village as if something spectacular was going to take place there as soon as my husband passed the B. Ed. exam (which eventually he never could). He was famed to be the only BA of the area and was a big shot in those days.

At my father's village I used to receive my husband's letters once in a while which, since I was illiterate, I had to get read with the help of my friends in the village. For reading those letters we had to go to the attic of my father's big and spacious house. The girls – naughty and talkative -- teased me in every which way while reading those letters. They even fabricated and added a few romantic sentences or adjectives from their own side in the letter. I tried to relish the subject matter of letters but was not hopeful that anything great was going to happen. Because I had come to know my husband's basic DNA, the genome.

"Once he had been to our village, for a day hardly. I was having my only son – a baby – then, that's you. The nieces of mine teased my husband saying that his son's countenance resembled his father's, to which, he remarked unwittingly, "A mango tree would bear a mango fruit only!" The little innocent girls blushed at this unseemly remark. Then I realised that my husband was not mature enough to tackle social interfaces, particularly, with female folk. He seldom visited my village thereafter, neither on any ceremony, nor on any other occasion.

He ultimately plucked in B. Ed.; and in the wake of that failure was a bitter failure throughout his life thereafter.

XXX

15. Feudal Philosophy: Getting Married, Begetting Babes!

Enter Protagonist

On the roof of my *Naanaa's*

sprawling buildings, beside the attic when my mother used to listen to the supposedly love letters from her husband through the instrumentality of hardly literate nieces of hers, I noticed that those naughty girls paid little regard to the fact that a babe was around, that is, me. I was fully conscious of the implications and meanings of their erotic conversations and teasing language directed towards my mother. It was clear from their histrionics and overacting during the reading of the letter that they interposed fabricated language and sentences in the contents of the letter to make the atmosphere more erotic and merrier for themselves as well as for my youthful mother. However, I suppose, there was nothing sort of erotic in those letters, for my father knew it well that my mother was an unlettered lady; and was thus obliged to take the help of other girls for deciphering the letter.

Somewhere I harboured a notion that the girls – who were quite older to me – ought not to have behaved in that fashion in my presence, that is, in the presence of a baby: a baby is not supposed to be exposed to eroticism becoming of the adults and grown-ups. I hence felt embarrassed at such moments and my mother often shooed me away from the scene. Life is like that: not every reality is supposed to be disclosed to everybody.

One recurrent rant that my mother was heard making at such instances was against my grandfather. She was not infrequently heard complaining that her father-in-law was an indolent, inactive person, that he did not do any physical labour, quite unlike her own father, that is, my *Naanaajee,* who was ever busy in this or that chore of the household, and of the agricultural fields. As against this, my grandfather, hailing as he did from a feudal set-up, did think it below his dignity to dirty his hands in such jobs as agricultural work or household chores. He virtually didn't do anything: and I wonder that was construed as greatness on his part.

My mother thought that it was my grandfather who was responsible for the culture of indolence in the family, particularly, my father. Had the grandfather been an industrious person like other villagers, my father would have naturally picked up the good habit of laboriousness. The mother was obviously peeved at the pathetic financial and social condition of her in-laws' household, particularly, of her husband, who was a super duper inactive and indolent person and took pride in not doing anything at all. For him and my grandfather, my mother and her elder sister – who was also wedded in that family only – used this couplet:

Rahe sukkha, mare bhukkha!

(meaning thereby, to rest in comfort, despite suffering the pangs of hunger!)

Actually, the financial well-being was nowhere in the consideration and reckoning of family members while designing a household; they could at the most think of getting married, getting dowry and begetting the maximum number of babes.

XXX

16. Whither 'Atithi Devo Bhava?'

Enter Protagonist

In my childhood at our *Naanaa's* sprawling and expansive home I often observed that at the main gate of the mansion type house my mother used to receive a *Naayee* (barber) youth who was from our paternal village and was having his in-laws in a nearby village called *Baadaulee (Baardolee).* Being from a lower caste he was not permitted entry into the interior of the house and was permitted to talk to his aunt (my mother) only standing outside whenever he used to visit his in-laws at *Baardolee.* As was the convention those days, he used to visit and pay obeisance to the upper caste lady from his village, and also, possibly to show off to his relatives there that he was acquainted with such prosperous people. He actually was overawed by the grandeur and riches of our mother's parental side whereas on her in-laws' side the financial position was pathetic and wretched. And they – this young lad and his relatives -- were often articulate in expressing this wide chasm between the status of two sides, and wondered how my mother could have been married with a person of not so wealthy a family and in a feudal-minded society.

During such courtesy calls by a so-called lower caste person with an upper caste lady from his village at the main entrance of the mansion, sometimes our elder *Maamaajee* happened to arrive at the gate while going in for having his evening meal: he used to have his evening meal before the sunset, like all other persons of the family and the village. Those were the days of kerosene lamp, and electric light was not in vogue till then. *Maamaajee* was a towering personality and had a deep baritone in his voice. He cursorily used to enquire about the youth and the youth bowing down to him used to tell him that he was from the same village from where his aunt was, and that his in-laws were in the nearby village. And *Maamaajee* used to enter the house splendidly.

I used to view this bizarre reception of a visitor quite amusingly wondering what type of social set up it was where a person visiting the family was received and stopped at the gate! This was in stark contrast to the dictum of *'Atithi Devo Bhav!'* as enunciated in the *Hindoo shaastras*.

XXX

17. My Previous Birth Or Death

Enter Protagonist

Till I attain *Arhatship*, the most coveted enlightenment, I am not going to be able to recall events beyond my present life-span. That is the boundary line of the memory for a creature endowed with a physical body in this Creation. They say, an *Arhant* may recall the events of even of his previous lives: the *Buddha* was able to recall all his previous incarnations, some of which, he even related to his *Bhikkhus,* the disciples from time to time. Those tales of recollections – *Jaataks* -- are quite interesting as well as instructive in effect. Nevertheless, I can set off recollecting the last moment of my previous birth, too. Unbelievable yet true, if I am not under delusion!

Lying moribund on a cot of straw strings, there is an old man in a far off interior village. He is sick, even as, senile by that stage or age. He is without any support in the form of family members: he has none left by this age, all have left for their next abode or existence already. Seems, it's his last moment in this life-span. Village folks – ladies and gents – have surrounded him on all sides, showing concern, sympathy and pity. The old man is alone at this old age; that's why they say, one must have family members to take care in one's old age. That's why *Shaastras* averred that *'Pun naam Narakaat Taarayate Iti Putrah'* (पुन्नाम् नरकात् तार्यते इति पुत्र:) (One who saves one from the agony of loneliness in one's old age is a son!). And, since girls go to other houses on getting married, it's only the lads who are of any consequence in that respect. 'The son is the ladder for heaven,' the saying goes. Not that there is any abode above; rather, to be under the care of one's family members in such eventualities as illness and old age is nothing short of divine blessing -- heavenly – indeed. To be uncared for in old age – why only old age, at any age, for that matter -- is infernal in old age, especially.

"Wretched old man! No one to take care of! Will pass away, possibly in no time," someone exclaimed and sighed.

"Oh, if only his only daughter could be called at this last moment! She could see the living face of his father for the last time," squeaked yet another kindly female voice.

To find all those acquaintances around my cot even in such a pathetic state I felt somewhat relieved: at least they were there to take care of my dead body, my corpse, to dispose it off. I long for my only daughter who is married and lives in some village far off and I express my consent for the suggestion of the second lady. In my state of semi-consciousness, semi-awareness, semi-faintness, I understand that there is some move towards sending for my daughter as soon as possible. Though 'possible' was to be viewed in the context of technological as well as scientific backwardness of those olden days coupled with the geographical aloofness of the habitat under mention. 'Soon' as well meant at least 'two or three days'.

I ruminate that even if my daughter arrived before my death, it made little difference for me. It would only add to the grief of separation for my daughter to see her father breathing his last before her eyes. And she being totally helpless in this respect! A feeling of looming relief pervaded whole of my existence at that juncture: 'now I shall die, there shall be no more rigmaroles and vicissitudes of life anymore! All the questions of this chapter of life will be meaningless and of little consequence, making no difference whether they were solved or remained unresolved.'

Even as I was awaiting arrival of my only offspring and hoping to die only after her arrival, suddenly I found myself on the entirely different platform – a scenario, shorn of any language -- the instrument of communicating my will and desires – totally incapable bodily. I could recollect, a moment ago I was part of another scene. Where are they all now? What would be happening there? Did my daughter arrive before I died? How would she have felt? I craved for those acquaintances bitterly. I longed for enquiring of those ones from these new ones -- the strangers. But I had no language; I did not know how to talk to them. I was devoid of all the faculties of human anatomy, which a little while ago I was so profusely endowed with. I took pity on those who would be mourning my death – both related ones and unrelated ones, although in that deserted village, no one might be called 'unrelated'! Where have I come? I cannot go back now. At least to console those people! To convey to them that nothing to worry about, that I am born again – reborn at some other place. Here at this place! At the same time! And these people are very happy. They are in a mood of celebration – merry-making. At my birth? Or at their gain? It is immaterial whether it is me or anyone else who might have come here instead of me! Nature has done well by making arrangement for obliterating the old memory from the current chip of

life, otherwise I would have continued my lamentations throughout my new birth and life.

I can't say how long this memory of my past birth, rather death, remained with me after my new incarnation. But it resurrected itself once I started practising *Vipassana*. The realisation that I was not under any delusion but having the memory of my past birth as I have narrated above came about very convincingly to me during my *Vipassana* practices.

XXX

18. The Earliest Memory

Enter Protagonist

The earliest memory that I have of my babyhood is a scene wherein my mother has arrived at her father-in-law's, from her father's home. I am in her lap, in her embrace. I am probably her only offspring at that time, and obviously so. She loves me a lot: that feeling is palpable in my heart. Her embrace affords me life sustenance and energy. Her in-law's is a vast compound bounded by rooms on all sides, inhabited by female folk of all stamps, as is usual in a joint family. There are old ladies, adult women, young lasses and kids – quite an assortment. The more the members of family, the more the merriment and sign of well-being.

Coming as my mother did from her father's just now, she is

beckoned by adolescent lasses to their side on the pretext of longing for their nephew – me -- from the lap of my young mother. My mother crosses over to their side of the vast *Baakhar* (female residences) and I find myself being passed over from my mother's lap to those of the adolescent aunts of mine. A palpable realisation of fear grips me at the time of my changing laps wondering if those lady folks would take ample care in this process not to drop me on the floor inadvertently. At that stage of my development I did not know that a baby is caressed with utmost care possible by his mother and near and dear ones, and also, that any inadvertent hurt to the baby hurts them more than the baby itself.

I remember being passed from one person to the other one by one, and there was lot of merriment on account of me: I was the centre of their merriment at the moment in a sense. I felt so pampered as though I was a very special creature. But this notion is misplaced. Not me but the fact that they had a baby – any baby, for that matter - was the cause of their merriment. Not me but the realisation that they had got a nephew – nascent one -- was the cause of their merriment. Also, behind the extra enthusiasm of the girls was the latent feeling that they wanted to impress their new sister-in-law, the wife of their brother, by showing love to her baby son, so that she might think that the girls were her well-wishers. One can show more love to someone by loving one's offspring. People love their offsprings to be loved more than themselves by others. If one intends to impress someone effectively, first of all one should enquire about the well-being of that person's children and their progress in various fields before setting off on any further discussion. This is a crucial piece of advice in social education.

XXX

19. *Death Undisclosed To A Baby*

Enter Protagonist

Yet another babyhood memory that I can recollect is that of my liking for an old person with an oval face, an affectionate face. He took me in his caressing hands with an enrapturing smile and coddling laughter and put me on his shoulders, my legs astride his neck. I used to crave his caresses and coddling. I didn't know his identity, though, nor was that phenomenon within the capability of my faculties.

But after sometime, he was conspicuous by his absence from the scene around me -- my dear chum. Used to his caresses and affection as I had grown, I craved his company and looked around for his entry all around me. But he was not to come, he was seen nowhere anymore. I wondered where that affable, kindly and affectionate face had vanished, had been lost. What had happened to him or me? What phenomenon was this disappearance of my favourite person called? Helplessness of a baby body: without a language, shorn of all the faculties to enquire, yet fully conscious of the happenings taking place around him; also, conscious of his longings! Only whatever is expressed by means of voice or language is not the only truth, whatever is felt inside the body is the real truth, reality indeed, irrespective of whether that may be expressed or not in words and through a man-made language.

Nobody had explained to me the phenomenon of his sudden departure from the scene of drama of my life — possibly the phenomenon of Death, that ubiquitous and ultimate reality of this Creation -- the *Sankhaar Lok* -- not only of the planet Earth, but the entire Cosmos.

However anxious as I was for this loss of pleasure of a baby's life, I can recollect one day I had found myself lying on a small cot -- of hardly two by two by dimensions, called *Peedhaa* (a distortion of *Sanskritic* term *Peeth,* to sit upon). Nobody was around, I wondered, a phenomenon which was quite abnormal by my experience of life thus far. Thus far I

had been carrying the impression that I was always invariably in the care of someone or the other of the family members, my well-wishers, or my lovers, so to say. But this was the first shock of my life. When I was left uncared for! What would have happened? So crucial as to leave even a baby unprotected or uncared for!

However, around me in the meantime emerged on the scene one young lady who was very familiar to me. She was my elder *Buaa,* eldest sister of my father – I was not aware in that state, of course. She found me wide awake on the *Peedhaa* and got startled. Wondering to see that I was neither crying nor making ruckus of any kind! She had expected me to be lying fast asleep as she was commissioned on the task by the family elders to my place only to ensure that I fell asleep. She began petting me and rhyming amorphously *'Aahaahaa.., sojaa.. sojaa.. Laalaa..'* blah blah... Her face and eyes were sad, morose, mourning as she did the death of our affectionate *Baabaajee*, the same affectionate persona, the elder brother of my real grandfather. That affectionate soul was no more around now! I had been deprived of the first love affair of my life! I could relate the morose mood and face of my caretaker at that moment with the likely demise of my fondness. 'That's why he is not seen of late!' I contemplated vividly if only I could not express it.

This mute realisation filled me with utter grief and I did not like to sleep anymore. But my *Buaa* was intent on making me sleep as was her brief assigned her by the family elders: to ensure that I kept sleeping come what may, irrespective of whatever might be a baby's psyche!

When I didn't fall in line with her wishes, she shook me irritatingly and even slapped me softly which was the first phenomenon for me of humiliation of a baby at the hands of a well-known acquaintance, a supposed well-wisher. I could not imagine in the mind of a baby, an innocent creature, if a young woman could shake a baby violently so as to make it sleep. I used to think thus far only that the babies could only be showered with affection, nothing else. But indeed this notion is not correct: babies are also beaten, humiliated, abused and subjected to all sorts of cruelty and punishments without remorse when it comes to the personal inconveniences or whims of the family elders.

I resolved mutely that I would keep in my memory the bitterness, rudeness and wickedness of this lady who apparently acted as my well-wisher before her brother and sister-in-law but in reality it was not so; that she behaved cruelly when all alone with the baby of another lady.

When I still did not sleep and instead started to beam at her so as to make her show me some love as was my wont, she did not flinch from her furious face and took me on her lap and set off towards the gloomy scene where the dead body of my favourite old man might be lying. I felt pleased to think of my getting to see my dear old man, and probably to assert my conviction that he was dead.

However, before I could witness this so far unknown phenomenon – of death -- for the first time with my own eyes, there on the way, the lady came across my lovely, young mother who grasped me in his lap affectionately. The lady carrying me irritatingly so far, suddenly changed tack and rather exhaled a piteous sigh, 'Poor baby, he has been uncared for long and also without milk for quite some time! Do take care!' and she kissed me on my cheek, too. Queer behaviour on the part of adults! What was the reality of their behaviour even they might not be knowing!

As everybody around was mourning and this was evident from their wet eyes, full of tears, I could make out that this was nothing but the mourning for the old man's demise; that he was no more!

However, I kept on feeling that these adults of the family should have shown me the dead body of my affectionate *Baabaa* so that I did not remain puzzled as to his status long thereafter. Had I seen him dying and being carried away on a pier I would have been certain that he was no more to be expected on the scene. That simple initiative on the part of adults would have cured me of my lifelong anxiety about the sudden disappearance of someone so favourite to me from the drama of my life. But the so-called adults in their pseudo wisdom could not think on those lines. Nobody had prepared them to live on those sane and sensible lines. Perhaps my narrative would give them a clue as to the upbringing of babes!

XXX

20. *Realisation Of Death As An Inevitability*

Enter Protagonist

The first ever realisation of death's inevitability dawned on me quite early in my babyhood itself, I think. It's the incident of *Kaakee*'s demise that forms the first episode of my tryst with the phenomenon of death: the memory of death! The arousing of awareness about the inevitability of death! That constituted my first tryst with the phenomenon of death. I would have been quite young at that age.

The spur for this realisation was the scene of death of *Kaakee,* the wife of *Kaakaa,* the two elderly persons – a couple -- who had been living in our village, at least at the time of my babyhood; later, when I came to senses, they were not found there anymore. They had died -- both. *Kaakee*, of course, died when we were innocent toddlers only.

On one such normal evening, when playing around, we overheard the elders of the family talking in hushed voices that *Kaakee* was dying. *Laado Kaakee* as she was fondly addressed was bed-ridden, lying there moribund within her hut, counting the last remaining breaths of her wretched life – as though having an interaction with her death before accompanying it. Without, we little kids were making merry, playing, indulging in childish quirks.

As soon as we came to know of this secret code, we started chanting in chorus, "*Kaakee* is dying! *Kaakee* is dying! *Kaakee* shall die by today evening!"

Kaakaa and *Kaakee* actually lived beside, rather beneath, the elevated platform of the land of the houses of our ancestors. They were sort of family members, yet aloof in a sense. Our childish reverie was, however, interjected by family elders when they upbraided us for this unseemly reverie on the inauspicious occasion of *Kaakee*'s death.

"Shut up! Rascals!", someone had chided us

remorselessly as well as mercilessly. We, the children, could not fathom this conundrum – the rebuke by the elders, for no fault of ours, in our perception. We were simply propagating the prophecy advanced by our parents and elders only concerning *Kaakee*'s imminent demise alike the hawkers of the newspapers.

We could not fathom the import of getting flogged like that at the hands of elders. We wondered in our childish fancies why the elders – the people – intended to suppress a truth, an inexorable happening to be? They probably did not like that the information about *Kaakee*'s death, which was to take place inevitably a few moments later, should be circulated a few moments in advance.

Nonetheless, we felt from their overall demeanours that they were pleased, too – maybe contemplating that if *Laado Kaakee* did die eventually, a big nuisance would be gone, implying thereby that with the demise of *Kaakee* the place or land on which they were inhabited, on which their hut was set up, would finally be vacated.

We saw *Kaakaa* standing there, brooding and sobbing, too. Thereafter only, we could realise that death was something to be feared of and something to abhor, and not a matter of laughing or merry-making. Also, we then realised that *Kaakee,* after dying, would no more be available for interaction or chatting with, like, she was available at that moment, and also, was a butt of our fun and pranks quite often. Both *Kaakaa* and *Kaakee* were the butts of jokes for all and sundry at the village, not only for us innocent kids.

Kaakaa and *Laado Kaakee* were very simple hearted folks. Eating rough and raw, and exerting to their full capacity: these were the tenets of their life-style. Other than this, there seemed to be no other specific aim of their lives.

I reminisce, once my father having brought *Kaakaa* to our dwelling unit, the intention being to feed him the *Pooye* (sweet cutlets) of *Ghee* (purified butter). My mother had prepared tasty sweet dishes called *Pooye*: in some specific style or manner. *Kaakaa* even as he was a plain hearted simpleton having never before tasted such savouries as my mother had prepared, got exceptionally moved and overwhelmed by this unbidden gesture on my parents' part. Expressing his heart-felt gratitude, he uttered stutteringly with a voice choked with emotions, *"Aley Chhundal! Telee bahoo to balee uchchyaar ai!"* (*Eh Sundar!* Thy wife is pretty smart and skilful!). Having got this testimonial of excellence and skilfulness in confectionary from *Kaakaa,* my mother felt as if she had made a great achievement in her life; for *Kaakaa* resembled and acted like the mythological *Naarad Muni*, *a la* a modern day correspondent – a journalist – for the hamlet: he used to spread the gossips as well as meaningful information – praise or slender -- throughout the village by word of mouth within no time. The result was that the information that my mother was a good household confectioner of sweet *Pooye* also spread far and wide in the village.

But to what avail was all this fame after all? On the contrary, it turned out to be a costly affair, a losing proposition, a dearly bargain. The acquaintances started expressing desire to eat *Pooyas*; in fact in a small village there is little distinction between a blood relation and a stranger; entire populace of the hamlet is akin to kith and kin only. There was, therefore, no question of charging something from anybody for the cost of sweetmeats offered thus; in countryside selling the eatables is a taboo; on the contrary, everybody had got to be fed gratuitously and sumptuously. Nevertheless, my mother's household was not a commercial restaurant which could benefit from this sudden upsurge or boost in the goodwill resulting, in turn, in the increased sales of merchandise. Lo, this was the difference between the then prevailing joint family set up and the modern day system which veers round and centres around but the money only!

We little kids had got to be rebuked exceptionally harshly by family elders for broadcasting the incident of *Laado Kaakee's* death in an unseemly as well as mirthful way if only innocently. Resultantly, we were obliged to ponder over the issue more seriously, and finally, to reach the conclusion that broadcasting death of anybody whosoever in a childish and mirthful way was not a doable thing. This we were realising for the first time in our short stinted lives! Nonetheless, the fact that the elders took serious objection to our child-like actions in the wake of the death of even such a trifling existence as that of *Kaakee* or *Kaakaa* whose lives didn't matter at all for these strongmen of the society, did baffle us children to wonder if their death was a matter of grieving, too. We were after all toddlers only! The death will therefore ever assume a status of nightmarish experience only – alike a very obvious reality – however, extremely dreadful. The man will never be capable of discoursing on the topic of death with an open and fearless mind.

Kaakee, the legendary figure, nonetheless, did die only after sometime of our supposed misdemeanour, done in the manner of declaring her death in advance, rather, as a prophecy. The only son of *Kaakee* did weep and wail pathetically, we observed. *Kaakaa* too, despite all his elderly hesitation, was finding himself incapable of checking his heart-felt sobs and tears. How mournful a scene it was, in the wake of a living creature's departure who supposedly seemed to be someone's very own! How fictional in fact all this is! This was the first time! In my living memories of current birth cycle!

The man does weep and wail on the death of someone – simply owing to the realisation that the fanciful dreamland of the ephemeral edifice of what is so adorably called life has eventually collapsed! Possibly ruing one's follies as to why one did continue to dream fancifully throughout one's life – a fantastic world, which didn't have any significance or substance in absolute terms!

When I returned home after playing, I was apprised that *Kaakee* had indeed died; also, we could hear for ourselves the mourning cries of the village women, and also, of the men folk, followed by several rituals being done before disposing of the mortal remains of old *Kaakee*. *Kaakee* was quite of an advanced age worth dying, still people were mourning, we toddlers were dumbfounded to think. Then what must be the age fit for dying when people would not mourn the death of their beloved ones? We were musing, we kids amongst ourselves. It is in the wake of this saddening realisation as well as contemplation that someone told me that all of our elders including parents must die one day; also, that we shall die too. And the most astonishing aspect to this piece of information was that the day of death might be any day, even today. That the death was just round the corner! It was indeed heart-rending. All of us who seem to be so real otherwise may die anytime without any warning or signal even!

That night I asked my mother whether she was included in that list, too. And she asserted in affirmation getting bemused.

That night thereafter I could not sleep. The prospect of my mother dying any moment kept on haunting me whole night. I wept, sobbed and prayed to God almighty: 'may my mother not die ever!' I shuddered at the thought of my mother dying during my childhood leaving me an orphan; what would happen to me in that eventuality? Oh God, save my mother, I cannot live without my mother! A baby's whole existence is badly dependent on one's mother's love and affection and caresses. A motherless child, an orphan, is deprived of a whole chunk of life's nectar in a sense.

I can remember still today that I was quite perturbed at this mortal thought of death, that the world as we see it is not substantial, it is virtual in a true sense. I would die too, another dreadful thought kept on haunting me for days together thereafter.

I prayed to God, 'O Almighty, I must die before my mother dies leaving me to feel the pangs of grief at her death. At least grant this prayer so that my mother must die after I am no more in this world -- in this present life-form.'

In the hindsight, presently, I can vividly see that my prayer offered to God during the babyhood had been granted as my aged mother is still alive and I am alive, too. Well, I had also added in my prayer to God that if in case my mother preceded me in dying, I must by then attain a mental level of a mature person who does not mind the dying of one's parents, mother included. That prayer has also been granted, for now I am in a totally dispassionate state of mind as regards the death of my mother. It will make no difference if she dies now at the ripened age of almost 92 years inasmuch as I know it is inevitable, however long she may live, or I may wish her living long!

XXX

21. Hunger Beneath The Mounts Of Cereals

Enter Protagonist

An anecdote verging on the cruelty as well as hypocrisy of human society concerning *Kaakaa* and *Kaakee* is worth relating here in the wake of their death.

Which caste or creed *Kaakaa* and *Kaakee* belonged, it's unknown, but it's well known that they had been dwelling amidst the habitations of our ancestors for long. Maybe they had sought shelter under the tutelage of our ancestors having come from some distant shore of a village; or it may also be the possibility that they might have come handy for this family at some time of emergency and need, obliging the chieftain or head of the larger family so as to keep them under his shade.

For them, on the lower side of the elevated land of the female residences, a thatched hut had been allowed to be set up. The dwellings of the owners of the land were built on the highlands – the *Khedaa*. Those were *kutcha* homes, too, no doubt; whereas back in Europe the humans had made long strides on the road of progress, here in our country still they allowed the natives to be confined to the outer limit of *kutcha* habitats only. The pucca bricks were not in vogue anywhere yet.

Just above the thatched settlement of *Kaakee* and *Kaakaa* there was a granary of cereals – a reservoir of grains – whose capacity was in hundreds of mounds, or quintals in modern parlance. The quantity of cereals stored therein was enough to satiate the hunger of multiple thousands of wretches. And, of course, it did do that job, too, that of satiating the hunger of thousands of wretches in the eventuality of food shortages. The grapevine has it that one of our contemporary ancestors was wont of catching hold of – inviting -- any passer by whosoever who happened to chat with him on the way, and fed him sumptuously; almost daily. Possibly this granary was the inspiration behind his proclivity towards altruism as regards offerings of food to the needy.

On the one hand, whilst there was so much store of food grains stocked there, there only, beneath the same granary both *Kaakaa* and *Kaakee* – the oldie duo – were obliged to spend their chilling wintry nights going to bed quite often without food. The fact of the matter is that the social set-up itself was framed like that; so that no body other than the members of the family of the strongmen could have food to their fill, and could be forced to behave obsequiously before them. The implied aim of the social system was that only, i.e.; to wield control by rendering a majority as wretches and keeping them hungry.

Why did *Kaakaa* and *Kaakee* suffer the pangs of hunger whilst in the village as a whole there was plenty of – rather, excessive -- stock of food grains and cereals? No need to break one's skull for cracking this puzzle at all! Only the writ of a single family would run – their *Manu-Samhitaa* only would be applicable! The tendencies and feelings that arise owing to Nature's workings and that ought to be the rules and regulations for guiding the human societies, are meaningless in the real world. If one is hungry, one has to suffer: what's queer about that? That seemed to be the thinking.

During one of such winter seasons, when *Kaakaa* and *Kaakee* found it hard to arrange *Rotee* for themselves – it was quite a normal phenomenon in those feudal days, in that multitudes didn't find it plausible to arrange *Rotee* for themselves and their families – *Kaakaa* and *Kaakee* struck upon a novel idea. It so happened once that *Kaakaa* and *Kaakee* could no more withstand the pangs of hunger.

In one such chilling and dark night of the winter season they cut open a small hole in the granary towards their plaintive hut; they broke into the wall of the granary stealthily near the bottom and made a small hole. From this hole, they took away some amount of grains daily and filled their empty stomachs. This judicious theft continued for entire wintry season, and nobody could suspect such a fine theft, more so, on the part of *Kaakaa* and *Kaakee,* who were the epitomes of virtues and righteousness! Of simplicity! And of selflessness!

Thereafter they spent whole of the winter season happily and merrily, with their stomachs filled for the first time to the full in their lives.

But when it was the time of harvest, and the spring season did arrive and bloom, the granary was eventually to be opened. When the granary was opened out of necessity after the winter season, that is, during the spring season, the adults of the household observed, to their amazement and bewilderment, a vortex created on the top of the grains: sort of whirlpool or a keep. To the utter astonishment of the owners; the level of the cereals in the storage had gone down.

On further probing, it transpired that there was a vortex, a pit at the top level of the cereals. How scientific a mechanism on the part of the Creator to notify the humans about the changes that might have occurred unbeknown to them! A godly device! Cereals did get stolen clandestinely by *Kaakaa* and *Kaakee* duo underneath in their hut, but on the upper surface the information got recorded by Nature regarding every minutest theft! Whatever amount of cereals had been stolen, the trough created on the surface was directly proportionate to that. Allegorically, as if the plain and pure conscience had been stained by gruesome misdeeds done secretively by *Kaakaa* and *Kaakee*, for that matter!

For a while, the mystery could not be fathomed, even as, they were simple rustic souls, unaware of the workings of natural science, or maths and geometry, as also, of the workings of the grey matter of the human brains. When the matter could not be resolved, they consulted literate persons like my grandfather who was one of the educated ones. He explained in plaintive terms that someone had stolen the grains, the cereals, from the bottom of the granary. This explanation was received but with ample amount of disbelief and scepticism. They could not be able to link it with any theft; for beneath the granary there was no question of theft, for no other than the persona of *Kaakaa* and *Kaakee* were dwelling there. How could a burglar break into the granary?

True, the burglar could not break into, but the watchman could do nevertheless! For, the reality was just the opposite; the trust had been breached; *Kaakaa* and *Kaakee* themselves had burgled into the granary. The fence itself had eaten up the harvest! However, my grandfather hushed up the issue by proffering the suggestion that for hungry people living beneath hundreds of mounds of cereals it is quite justifiable that they should break into it for satiating their hunger. Nobody on this planet has got any right to store the mounts of cereals on the heads of human beings whilst two souls were living with hungry stomachs just beneath that.

Caught did get *Kaakaa* and *Kaakee* and were reprimanded, too. Nonetheless, both of them averred nonchalantly and innocently, "We were dying of hunger. We eat whatever we get from your households only. Also, we do exert whatsoever only for you people. Still if we get to have starved, whose fault is it by the way?"

Possibly the words uttered did convey much more than they literally meant; the import was grave. The owners did absolve both of them; but as if to ameliorate their own sins or to hide their own crimes they rejoindered, "If that was the case, you had better ask for from us, why resort to stealing clandestinely?"

"My lords, what constitutes theft, what not, we do not understand; we had merely accepted the offerings of mother *Annapoornaa* (the goddess of granary). And that given by you folks on our asking for it would have been given as a condescension or as a debt after all! These morsels of food are but the

clots of our blood only! And see the irony, even we have no right to have them and eat them!"

XXX

Table of Contents

22. Compound Of Neighbours At Highlands

Enter Protagonist

The household where *Kaakee* and *Kaakaa* were sheltered – ensconced rather – beneath the upraised platform, the highlands, had quite a vast compound. Apart from the dwelling units – only *kutcha* and thatched ones, of course – of the various sub-units of the joint family – since divided under the pressure of advancing generations – there were quite a number of trees and saplings growing as well, which imparted the habitats perched on that highland quite an attractive view. Wherever there is a semblance of Nature's bounty, there is a natural feeling of pleasantness and soothing. Given the claustrophobic and suffocating atmosphere of our personal habitat, my parental habitat, where I always felt as though getting suffocated and depressed, without any ray of happiness and mirth, I felt naturally tempted to go play in the compound which was incidentally quite opposite our hut or home, whatever one would like to call it.

And to add to my mirth as though providentially, there was available a companion also, called

Angad, who was almost my age. He was of my age but not at the same rung of ranking in the context of relationships; he was my uncle. By body as well he was quite lanky and weak. Mirthful, too. And with these covenants present providentially I took him as my natural playmate, as if made for each other only. Otherwise, how could it be that he was my age; his house was opposite mine one; and he had a sprawling compound in his large household; and where we were permitted too to play our child-like games and to make mischiefs and noises!

His father was, however, an influential person if only a whit cunning and astute, reputedly a clever sociable personage: he was actually the chieftain *(Pradhaan)* of the village. Not only his innate traits, but also, his position in the social and administrative set up -- which he richly deserved in view of his natural traits – only went to aggravate his natural tendencies of a puffed up youth or adult as his age might have been. And a son's status and influence is determined in direct proportion to one's father's stature, so *Angad* had an upper hand in all our playful dealings and our occasional childish wranglings. It was always he who was favoured by his family members whenever we happened to squabble or wrangle on some trifling issue. He had in fact three elder sisters and was the only

son to his parents, that too, after an abnormal gap of almost a decade from the birth of the third sister. Obviously, he was the pupil of his parents' eyes. They could not brook any indecency in their son's prestige. At times when I took cudgels to teach him a lesson on some valid point when he was in the wrong, his family members came to his rescue, apparently upbraiding me – the child of not so prominent and influential a father, rather a deranged father.

Despite all the humiliation that was not infrequent and was ever invariably adversarial to me, I did not flinch from playing with this childhood chum, for I found the natural settings of his habitat – the small grove of vegetation – much precious than my own insignificant prestige. Nonetheless, somewhere in my psyche, even at that tender age, which is supposed to be the age of ignorance and stupidity, I could vividly perceive that the behaviour of those adult folks was not impartial; they behaved shamelessly in favour of their kith and kin. The trait of nepotism and favouritism is inbuilt in the DNA of the *homo sapiens* I strongly feel! Even at that age, I could realise so palpably that the phenomenon of relationships is but phony one, and has no real substance in it. When it comes to real test of supporting the blood relations entailing some personal or financial sacrifice, nobody comes forward; and every starving person has to die all alone, no one comes to feed one, out of one's platter of food.

XXX

23. Mother Asks If I Feel Hurt On Being Beaten

Enter Protagonist

Of my earliest memories, one that I could still today so explicitly recall is that of my covering my cheeks – soft crimson cheeks of a babe – from any prospective unsuspected assault by my enraged mother. I carried an incessant feeling in my heart that my mother could slap me without any provocation whatsoever from me – and her slaps did hurt me quite unbearably, her own assessments of her slapping being quite soft and benevolent notwithstanding. Besides, the psychic pain that was engendered in its aftermath, was all the more incarcerating – to think as to what for I had been punished; most of the time, it was her ill-behaved husband who was the indirect cause of her anguish and the brunt was to be invariably born by me – the unprotected, unharmful baby! If crying wasn't devised as a means to rid oneself of such unsolicited pains and misfortunes by the Creator of this queer Creation, the world would have been rendered inhabitable by such insensitivities of parents.

One day, the day of my beatings – for what fault of mine, I didn't know – when I was tramping around in our hutment – the only room that formed the abode of husband of my mother – on seeing my mother approaching me I put both my hands on both of my chubby cheeks. I was afraid that the cruel and mindless mother could again hurt me – because it was so easy and so mirthful to beat the innocent babies. Possibly moved by this feat of mine or probably taking pity on me by grace of God on me, she caressed me this time lovingly and sitting on her folded legs so as to come to my level while talking – because I was so small – she asked me in motherly tone, *"Laalaa,* do you feel hurt when I beat you?" as though she did beat me for giving me pleasure and pain to herself; any fool could have surmised that it hurt me when she beat me, hurt me not only bodily but all the more psychologically.

Still, as if taking pity on her so as not to accentuate her pain, I lied that it didn't hurt me at all.

Actually, when I responded to this effect, I had in fact forgotten the particular beating to which she had alluded her question at that moment.

But I can recall succinctly still that it was on those days when I got beatings at the hands of my mother when her husband beat her on this excuse or that, the intrinsic value of which I could never fathom until this day -- when I have come to realise that it was owing to his daily as well as unreasonable demand for money put on my mother. He was an egoist sort of man, an ostentatious man; he taught in a nearby town and there amidst his teacher colleagues he showed off, sort of bantered, that he was the progeny or scion of a well-to-do family, rather, from a feudal society. That was a half-truth, of course; he was exactly so, but as for his individual capacity, he was a pauper, an indolent and misguided youth, a good for nothing creature. He depended for even a single paisa on his wife's scanty stock which she collected from her father's side as farewell presents. This situation was very shameful indeed! But her husband, that is my father, was such a rogue! Such an indolent creature!

XXX

24. First Realisation Of My Growth

Enter Protagonist

By now as a babe I harboured the notion that I was a small creature – small bodied – forever; and should remain as such -- at the mercy of others, so to say. How ignorant I was and everybody is in babyhood!

In the name of home, at our father's side, we had only half a room – that too, *kutcha* walled and thatched one. The impression being harboured in my mind of being a scion of wealthy and grand pedigree notwithstanding! That shared room – shared with our elder aunt, the wife of my father's elder brother – had no almirahs or wardrobes or cupboards in modern day parlance; it merely had a few niches: and of course a bigger niche on which important items of household could be put. This niche had a protruding platform; my height was just to fit me under its shade. I had the impression that my height was fixed, unchangeable and that I was destined to stand only under that terrace for good.

Nonetheless, one day when I was roaming in my hutment – that is, the single room, rather the shared half room, *kutcha* room – I reached up to the cornice, rather, niche in the wall, on which, most of the daily usable articles were kept. I found to my amazement that on raising my hand I could reach the articles kept there. Here-to-fore, I could not reach them, though for past sometime I was having an inkling that I was reaching a bit higher every time I raised my hands. By that time I had not come across any such phenomenon as 'growth' of animate beings.

When I observed this queer occurrence, I could not help yelping and calling my mother who was my only companion of pleasures and sorrows. *"Beebee!* I have reached this high! Look!" For me, this was an eighth wonder; for mother, it was nothing! Simply a truism! But realisation of even this truism to a babe is a great incident indeed, I realised. Mother betrayed pleasure to amplify my pleasures which were very few and far between. She possibly also added that I was growing well. Thenceforth I gained ample confidence and belief that I was growing constantly and should grow to the heights of my mother and my tyrant father in due course one day. This feeling gave me tremendous amount of perverse pleasure and confidence, to be frank.

This seemingly trifling phenomenon of 'Growth' caught my fancy, sort of; I would by and by stand by my mother's side and measure my height against hers, and every time there was some improvement I derived tremendous amount of satisfaction and yelled, 'I am growing!'

Growth, that is, change is such a permanent feature of the Creation! This fact took time to be implanted in my psyche. Also, there is the reversal of this entire process, that is, Decay, which I am coming to realise presently when I am growing old and ageing: still growing; yet too much growth implies decay. That is nature's norm! This implies completing the perfect cycle!

Gradually, I came to realise that now I was able to pick things kept on the terrace with my hands; earlier I was not able to do so: I had to beseech my mother for picking something from there. After few more months I was able to raise my head and shoulders above that niche. It was an amusing mystery for me: I was gaining in height! My mother was very encouraging by nature.

This way, I came to know of the phenomenon of continuous growth of living beings including human beings and the resultant growing height: it never remains the same, I realised. It keeps on changing every day, every moment like all other phenomena of the cosmos!

XXX

25. Naanee's Snoring & Getting The Stolen Guavas

Enter Protagonist

Of almost the same time period is the following memory.

I have reached *Nanihaal* with my mother and am probably quite a babe by that time. My *Naanee* is glad to see her darling daughter come home on visit to her parents' village. All the more glad is she to see her grand-children – the children of her youngest daughter.

When the night falls, we go to bed; and I am eventually made to sleep with my *Naanee*. First day it's okay somehow, even as, throughout the night I am troubled by *Naanee*'s snoring. The next day, at the time of going to bed I complain to my mother, to the amusement and laughter of all, that I do not want to sleep with *Naanee* 'because *Naanee*'s nose creates lot of noise throughout the night'. I could not fathom why I was not being made to sleep with my mother as usual. Actually, my mother had begotten yet another baby and my privilege to sleep with my mother had been taken over by that baby – my sibling; I was now shorn of that privilege; that is the fate of every privilege whatsoever, I realised in later life, however.

Naanee chastised me mockingly and offered me some interesting story as an inducement for my sleeping away from my mother and for agreeing to sleep with herself. I was obliged to acquiesce in the end.

In the same situations I often got to have ripe, fresh guavas brought by my maternal uncle from the nearby orchard, of course, procured stealthily, that is, without any consideration, to the consternation and complaint of the gardener – the owner or the contractor of the fruit orchard. But in those days, and in those areas in the rustic environs, the theft of fruits and vegetables was not considered an offence or a sin or even a moral hazard at all. And I ate the fruits of those *de facto* moral hazards without any qualms of conscience: the conscience I didn't have any at that age though; that was a later day formulation as well as imposition by the society.

Yet another intriguing as well as irritating activity in those days was the fondling with my sexual organs by my maternal cousin of almost my age or so. He was a kid too, but fond of fondling with urinating organ under the cover of quilt, or the covering sheet. I internally felt very irritated, yet for fear of elders that the fallouts of disclosing that misdeed might mar my friendship with *daadaa* and that it might tarnish the image of us both, or I don't know for what conception, I did not muster courage to bring this activity to the notice of the family elders. And suffered in consequence! The activity having metamorphosed into a bad habit of masturbation throughout my later life that I couldn't help despite my best intentions. The *sanskaars* created during the childhood have permanency in nature. How far I was accountable for this vice and how far the social set up influences one's habits – good or bad -- I can't decide even at this ripened age of mine. Another pertinent point is if at all the activity is bad?

XXX

Table of Contents

26. Latched Inside The Room Of Sweets

Enter Protagonist

For the joint family of my maternal grandparents was quite large, we had drawn an impression that there always took place at least one marriage in that household every summer season: almost every season, so to say, without exception. Or maybe in our child psyche we felt like that, given the fact that if not in our immediate relationship the marriage ceremony might be taking place in some other households closely related to our maternal grandparents. And marriage ceremonies were not like those celebrated nowadays – merely a spectacle of few hours and then one and all dispersed – ceremonies those days used to continue for months together, starting months before and stretching months after the rites proper. The relatives from far and near did arrive months in advance, especially, the lady folks; however, the menfolk did arrive weeks in advance still. Nobody seemed to be in dearth of time and nobody was in a hurry so as to run away immediately. There used to be an atmosphere of mirth and merriment all around, and also, that of unbreakable camaraderie. The affair used to be a common monetary affair in which every household used to contribute; it was not a burdensome chore for an individual, unlike, it is these days.

On one of such occasions of utter effusion and merriment, I found myself latched inside the room wherein the sweets and delicacies were kept stored. Well, it was the tradition those days that private confectioners were hired who prepared variety of sweets, dishes and delicacies for the occasion, and the items thus prepared were kept stored in a designated store house, a good tidy room. Not only this, there used to be designated a specific person, an in-charge for taking care of the room and its contents, and she – it was invariably to be a female and, that too, of a fairly advanced age – was called *'Kajaitin'* (the *kaaryakartrin*). My *Naanee* normally used to be the *Kajaitin* on all such occasions as I noticed; it was a cumbersome duty, laden with lot of responsibility, warranting alertness of highest degree, of course. And my *Naanee* discharged this duty gleefully as well as efficiently, even as, her countenance was naturally a smiling and effusive one.

It so happened on one such occasion that following in the footsteps of my *Naanee* I entered the room of sweets – maybe with a desire on subconscious level to have a piece of sweet dish – despite lack of faculty to express myself efficiently and clearly. I was of quite a younger age, it means. *Naanee*, however, had entered the room to fetch some dishes for some guest who had arrived only recently and someone – a male – was there to fetch those items to the guest. I being a small bodied creature was somehow hidden behind their big bodies, towards their backs, however unintentionally, and for I didn't have the faculty of speech yet developed to the full, I could not express myself or could not make my presence felt to the hosts duo. Also, I had the notion in my childish mind that the duo would take notice of their surroundings – my presence around them -- before leaving and latching the room from outside; and I engaged myself in picking the choicest dishes from the containers full of variety of sweets.

However, the two fellows hurried out without caring for the interior of the room and banged the thick and heavy wooden door and latched it from outside. I could not even shout that I was there 'IN'. The emotional shock for me the babe was so grave that my voice whatever I had choked and, instead of making noise, I started sobbing. The first thing I did was I threw away all the sweets into their respective containers. I had lost all desire to have them now; there loomed before me the spectre of life and death. Now how could I go out? I didn't have the faculty to communicate, that is, to speak out. Speech is such

a valuable faculty!

I reached the formidable wooden door crest-fallen, helpless. The enterprise to serve myself with delicacies had turned sour. What to do now? It was really a very big question, for a toddler. Now the next chance would be only when there would arise another demand for sweets outside, when some other guest would arrive; but that was no guarantee, for it was already the time of eventide.

However, as they say, adversity is the mother of invention. I started jerking the heavy door violently however I could, and I found that I could simultaneously make some noise too through the creaking of the wooden door, quite enough to draw the attention of the people laughing and chatting outside in the sprawling courtyard of the mansion-type house. I was filled with utter pique and anguish at that moment.

Nevertheless, the trick worked -- the child's contrivance. The unusual shuddering of the wooden door drew attention of the people eventually; first, they wondered what it could be, they thought it might be some dog or cat or even a monkey, for whoever it might be it was speechless if only a creature. Had it been the baby of a *homo sapiens* it would speak, but it didn't. They rushed to the door and unlatched it and pushed the door cautiously to open, only to find a baby of a *homo sapiens* inside, and the loveliest one: the toddler son of their dearest youngest daughter, the darling of *Naanee* herself. Everybody burst into loud laughter. They started teasing me by casting aspersions that I had entered the room surreptitiously so as to fill my belly with sweets; also, that I would have eaten so much sweets, and that the quantity of sweets in the containers that were filled had dwindled significantly since.

However, I was wondering that I was being accused of what I had not done; I had rather not touched even a single sweet to my tongue and had even emptied my hands of whatever I had picked in the first instance. In the eventuality of impending calamity my priorities had shifted from sweets to salvaging my existence somehow. My *Naanee*, however, out of pity and affection towards me, took me by hand and tried to give me some sweets, but I was so piqued at the hilarity of the adults and their callousness that I could not accept any sweet anymore even when offered by my beloved grand maternal mother -- *Naanee.*

The same desire that had arisen in my child heart had vanished in the face of calamity.

That was indeed a very horrible experience for me!

XXX

27. Facial Paralysis Of My Mother

Enter Protagonist

One crucial mishap possibly I have omitted. My mother used to grind cereals to make them into flour almost daily on the hand-driven stone grind-mill at home. That was the norm in those days. That provided enough physical exercise for the housewives in those environs of feudal captivities.

One day I felt that the mother was not grinding the flour, rather, there was a good deal of flurry all around in the small house, especially, around my young mother. Unbeknown to me, she was taken to her maternal home and confined to a pitched dark room – completely dark – in which possibly even air could not enter, to my child's mind. The room was in fact meant for storing grains, the harvest of the family. My mother was confined to that one, to my childish amazement, of course. But I was not aware at all of the gravity of the matter that my mother had been struck by a stoke of paralysis. Nobody had so much as thought of apprising me.

I had, however, accompanied her to the house of my maternal grandparents. The mother was given best available treatment in that area: it was only the local system of treatment, nonetheless.

I observed, however, that I

was not taken to my mother insofar as my mother's face had been twisted, and I might be scared by seeing that distorted figure, myself being a toddler only. But whosoever – their acquaintances -- happened to visit my ailing mother, after having paid a visit to the mother inside her captivity, invariably showed sympathy and pity towards me. Whereas I was not at all aware, neither of the calamity nor of its ramifications and their impact on my existence. However, when they treated me with so much affection and extra condescension I felt that I should have shown myself morose and melancholy.

However, as per conventional wisdom, my mother was administered, inter alia, the meat of pigeons as medicine to eat and possibly as a result, the mother was alright within a few weeks. Poor pigeons had to sacrifice themselves for vanquishing paralysis of my mother, alike sage *Dadheechi* sacrificing himself for vanquishing daemons – particularly *Vritra* -- at the instance of *Indra*. That was a grave calamity which my father could not have handled at all; rather, he shifted his responsibility to his in-laws. Such a worthless husband he was! My father did not think it as his duty to take upon himself the responsibility for anything connected with his family, except procreating babies! That, too,

was not intentional, rather, was the providential outcome of the intercourse between a male and a female in the wake of satisfaction of carnal lusts.

In the same breath let me reminisce yet another gory occurrence concerning my young mother that frequented itself regularly when she visited her parental house. She was hale and sundry, yet I found once in a while that she got fits of severe epilepsy wherein her teeth would be clenched tightly together, and she would lose consciousness; yet she shook herself very violently as well as precariously, lying on the cot or on the floor, like a fish out of water. That was a very frightful scene, and one could easily surmise that the lady was dying. I being a small child used to get frightened, too, for it was pretty possible that my mother could breathe her last in that process. However, the family elders – her paternal siblings – did not get frightened or alarmed; they instead busied themselves in holding her tight so that she would not fall off the cot and hurt herself. To resuscitate her and to help her regain consciousness, they made her smell the dirty footwears, to my utter amusement and bewilderment. In normal circumstances, no sane soul would do that! My mother was made to smell the obnoxious smell of filth stuck to the soles of the footwears.

That bizarre treatment I could never fathom! But that was working all along as per the experience of the family elders. And there would have been someone who might have invented that as the treatment for epilepsy or fits of young lasses. And they were resorting to that treatment. Also, *inter alia*, they closed the nostrils of the young lady in an effort for bringing her to senses quickly.

During this entire episode, my breath was stopped, too; and I kept on praying to I don't know whom that He should be kind enough so that my beloved mother might recover. When ultimately she used to recover her senses, she started behaving quite normally as if nothing had ever happened at all.

Now in the hindsight, I realise that the mental disorder was epilepsy and had something to do with the sexual activity; non-satisfaction of that. For my mother, instead of getting love of her husband, she was getting sticks on her back, and also, she was staying in her paternal home away from her husband. Whenever she might be feeling the sexual urge as per nature's dispensation, she might be getting those fits. Sexual urge is as natural as the nature's other calls, like, urinating and excreting.

However, in advanced age, I never saw my mother suffering those fits; that's only a disorder connected with the youth and the sexual urge. And sexual lust got satiated by smelling obnoxious smell of leathery as well as dirty footwears! Quite strange! In light vein, I at times think, that's why masculine genders use their *chappals* for beating the sexual offenders!

XXX

28. In The Garb Of A Child Bridegroom

Enter Protagonist

One of the earliest episodes of my current life is the memory of my being harnessed as the virtual bridegroom for *Mahendra Maamaa's* newly wed bride. The tormentor maternal uncle!

The scene comprises a rainy season: the rain has stopped and the weather is cool and sumptuous. The agricultural fields are lush green all around, interspersed with tall trees with heavy canopy of greenery – it was still not the time when human misery and greed had consumed every bit of a tall tree from the land. There were a few fields which were left uncultivated for the season -- this was the normal practice back then: to leave some fields open, uncultivated and unsown so that those could replenish themselves with fertility anew. The landholdings were quite large so as to afford this luxury of using and to spare too. These empty patches of land which were occasionally ploughed so as to keep the weeds away looked quite fit for playing various types of games for us kids.

I found myself being carried away by one aged lady towards a nearby village to my amazement and bewilderment. That hamlet consisted of hardly a dozen households. At one of those households there was sort of a ceremony going on. A fairly large gathering, mainly of ladies and young girls, was there – singing and merry-making. I being a toddler had a licence to intermingle with this assemblage of opposite sex, the fair sex — by that time I had not come to understand the dichotomy of sexes. A great deal of jollity was abound there. I could still sense that this was the house of one of our *Naanee's* and *Naanaajee's* close acquaintances.

After a while, I found myself tied in a knot with the *saree* of a veiled young lady, and the jolly gathering singing and merry-making beckoning me to move forward in the lead. I would be quite young, for I did not know the ABC of all this queer sort of ritual. The women started teasing me by remarking, "Here is your wife; you are her husband!" Me, husband! How come they have made me a husband: without even my knowing? I started feeling shy, shy by nature as I ever was. 'What is this non-sense. I do not want to be seen as a person having anything to do with sex.' I was musing, 'This is a matter of shame for me. To have anything to do with ladies or girls!' But they were in their highest reverie. I didn't even know the way to my *Nanihaal* from this village, hence an elder lady was catching me by finger and leading me onto the correct path. After sometime, I started enjoying this festivity and the unbidden honour I was endowed with. After taking almost an hour for a short journey through vast grounds surrounded by lush greenery, we reached *Mahendra Maamaa's* home and there, after solemnising various rituals, me acting as a virtual hubby to the bride in lieu of *Maamaa,* I was set free, of course, after giving me an honourable present.

After this incident, I found every which person teasing me reminding of this husbandry. I too started relishing after a short spell of shyness as if it were some matter of shame to become a husband. I wanted to become a recluse in life, in my subconscious mind, not having anything to do with female sex and family life.

XXX

Enter Protagonist

The village where we were headed was about 15 or 20 kms

away from our *Naanaa*'s village, headed towards which was our marriage party. I was prepared by my mother and one elder lady in *Maamaa*'s household for the first ever marriage party of my current life-span. The occasion was the marriage ceremony of the son of our elder *Maamaajee*'s eldest, rather the only, son. Being the eldest son and a scion of a wealthy family, he was called as *'Kunwar'* and was a very handsome lad at that time. He had left by train along with the other members of the marriage party. We were going by bullock cart: along a water channel called *Bambaa,* a brook. In the bullock cart, I was feeling safe and secure insofar as other children of somewhat greater age and height were accompanying me, too, along with the towering presence of my *Naanaajee* and some of his close relations, and of course the valuables, jewellery etc being carried for the ceremony. To protect those valuables and the children, there were some armaments as well, not necessarily fire arms, but lances and sticks etc. The concept of *Baaraat* (marriage party) would have been conceived exactly for this purpose: that is, to protect against any waylaying or plundering by predators on the way. The topography and the social milieu of the times bygone – dark days -- was not like that prevailing presently.

At that age, however, my impression of *Naanaajee* is not that of an affable person, a person who loves babies and children; he used to behave rudely with children, especially with me. I did not like him as such in the same sense as I liked my younger *Maamaajee*, who incidentally was also accompanying us in the bullock cart. How we managed the toilet related issues of a kid I do not know; that was the concern of elderly people. But throughout the journey, as also, on reaching the spot of sojourn, I felt like I was travelling through a wonderland: everything seemed new and amazing to me. For a child everything is new and amazing in the world! Like Alice in the wonderland!

Time at that age was also an elastic phenomenon and had the proportions of aeons, unlike at present age when even aeons seem to be like merely the fleeting moments. At the spot of stay, there was ample scope for playing and walking around, yet lots of restrictions were imposed by grown-ups upon us young ones. The time was not passing and we kids were becoming desperate to reach the village of marriage ceremony. As per tradition in those days, the marriage party could not reach directly the venue; they had to stay somewhere at a distance from the place, and from there in the evening, the marriage party was carried in bullock carts to the destination with fanfare and fireworks. Automobiles were a rare luxury, even buses were very few: those were called *'lorry'* and were a matter of awe for both children and old ones.

In the evening, the marriage party was taken as usual to the *Janvaas -- Jana-aavaas --* I being taken full care of by my maternal uncle and his sons. I needed not have to worry about myself! It was a joy to have feasts sitting on earth on jute strips! A deal of prestige was associated with being a *Baaraatee!* Lot of arrogance and tantrums apart! The people on bride's side were on receiving end no doubt.

Well, the anecdote of my elder *Maamaajee* must not be omitted: he was the father of the bridegroom and deserved to be the most prominent personage on the occasion. But, as told earlier, he was a crazy personality, full of queer tantrums. He did not accompany the *baaraat;* rather, he chose to first finish the household's chores at his village and then proceed towards the destination in the afternoon, well groomed, of course. People were getting nervous at the marriage site at the prospect of the father of the groom not having arrived, not being present.

And lo! There comes the father of the bride-groom, mounted on a camel's humped back. *Maamaajee* was a tall and handsome personality and sitting on the camel's hunch he looked all the more taller. That incident became a butt of joke in the marriage party. But everybody knew the temperament of our *Chhatrapaal Maamaajee* whose name was after our legendary ancestor *Chhatrasaal*!

XXX

30. Dhaand–Ballaa

Enter Protagonist

Obviously, I was a pampered baby at that time. There was nothing special about it. What I think is that my mother hailed from a well-to-do family and was well-behaved as well. Naturally, her first, lovely, child was to be shown extreme affection by all concerned. My mother would have been pretty as well, as I think, since that is also one of the factors for entitling babies for extra affection from the side of relatives and acquaintances which they show more towards the beauty not as much towards the baby or her baby. When I got kingly treatment from my uncle in the instance of blood-shedding of my little finger, I started harbouring a notion that the affection that he had shown towards me was everlasting and a normal phenomenon, also, that grown-ups love the babies and children.

Those were such kingly days of my life: when I was least aware of the time and space. One day, during the month of *Saavan* - the month of monsoon season – as was the convention, my mother slung a rope in the ring of my door and gave it the shape of a swing which was meant for my merriment as well as entertainment. I enjoyed the swinging like a fairy flying in the sky.

During that tenure, while on outing some paces away from the house, I happened to see children playing with a stick, a bat, and a ball, some sort of a game like cricket. They were beating the ball with the stick so as to make it run away and then some children chased the ball so as to catch it. When a child beat the ball, it made a sound of loud bang and out of mirth I happened to shout aloud, "*Dhaand! Ballaa!*" trying to emulating the amorphous sound and the cause of it. I wondered at the craziness of the boys musing: if at all they were intending to catch the ball why in the first place they did strike it so as to go far away. But all the actions of our living style are queer: everything comes to a naught finally; yet everything is longed, indulged in, and discharged with so much attachment and desperation! Only to come to a naught in the end!

The children around got amused at this queer expression of mine, and many of them resonated and repeated, "*Dhaand Ballaa!*" in my style. They joined the two disparate words and rendered it the shape of a motto. I saw pleasure and appreciation in my spontaneous invention and started chanting *'Dhaand Ballaa*!' myself repeatedly. I came home chanting the same *'Dhaand Ballaa'* and many grown-ups picked up this refrain – the peculiarity -- of mine as my speciality acquired from my previous birth. Some of them associated it with the notion that in my previous birth, I would have been a cricketer that's why I kept on shouting *Ballaa, Ballaa.* Being a child, I could but trust whatever the aged people were deducing from my actions. Nonetheless, I did not know what the matter was and what the reality was. '*Dhaand*' was *de facto* the sound made by the collision of the bat and the ball when it struck it; I simply picked that up and tried to emulate, to transliterate, the sound into words.

Later on, this peculiarity kept sticking with me and became my speciality, a trait of mine, for quite a long while. Whenever someone accosted me on the way, they invariably beckoned me with *'Dhaand Ballaa'*, as if *'Dhaand Ballaa'* was the mode of greeting me. And believe me, I thoroughly relished this new found glory that cost me nothing. Also, I realised how idiot the world of adults was!

XXX

31. Blood-Shedding Is Ephemeral, Too!

Enter Protagonist

Such trivial remembrances cannot be associated with any exact date when these occurred: only a rough idea is there in that going by the caressing – excessive caressing – behaviour of the grown-ups towards me at that time, I can vouchsafe that I would have been an infant or at the most a toddler.

In those days, the geography or the topography – to be precise – of our area, our countryside, was starkly different from what it looks like presently. The area abounded in palm trees, date trees and betelnut trees apart from coniferous trees, and such vegetation was aplenty. It appeared as if nobody was the owner of such vegetation found in the wilderness all around our village. The terrain was, too, mostly un-arable and rugged, rather, left over: as pastures for cattle for use by one and all. It was quite a field for enjoying freedom, particularly, for the children and babies. The beasts were absent, too, having been preyed upon in the British *Raaj* by the feudal lords and courtesy of fiefdoms.

One day, I happened to accompany my babyhood companions to the fields or wilderness – whatever you may call it -- which was actually hardly a few furlongs away from the village and was characterised by an orchard – a groove of mango dominated fruit trees. There I enjoyed the tantrums and errands of children: we climbed the low-height trees; we plucked local berries; we broke the twigs from soft plants; also, we mishandled the *Rahat* – the contrivance to pull water from the well dug up in the garden. After all that humbug, we started meddling with the sharp-edged and thorny bushes and grass, which in the beginning gave pleasure but ultimately when we exceeded our brief, it cut the soft skin of my little finger. The blood started oozing out from there and the scarlet colour of blood on any limb of the body was anathema for me by that time. Moreover, if cut once, how could it be stopped or closed! By that age, we kids were unaware of the nature's miracle and its benevolence in curing the bodies of animate creation. I started yelling – there might have been some feeling of pain as well, I cannot deny -- but primarily it was the shock of misgiving that once the blood started oozing out it would not cease ever. The companions as well showed panic in the equal measure. They rushed me – pulling by my arms -- towards the village, my home.

Yelling and shrieking to the amazement of one and all I reached home. Before my young mother could take care of my pitiable condition, one of her brothers-in-law, that is, one of my uncles took control of the situation. He first of all assured me in a care-free manner as if nothing serious had happened, "*Eh,* let me see; come on! Nothing, it's nothing, really! Let me apply the lotion and it will be all right within no time. Just see!..." *blah, blah...* More than the medication that he might have administered, his caressing and loving attitude soothed my feelings and the pain if at all there was any. I could realise in the process that the spilling of blood does not continue forever, it stops after a while like all the other things in motion. And later on, I realised too that if the blood of a creature is good and pure, it coagulates all the more quickly. My uncle was at work of dressing my small finger when he was doing all that loose talk that was warranted for taking care of my mental misgivings, for diverting my childish attention. Our world is created by our mind only!

Mind is more important for relieving the pain and agony: most of our sorrows are based on our ignorance and misconceptions. *Mano pubbangamaa dhammaa, mano setthaa manomayaa,* as lord *Buddha* has averred. (Everything whatsoever occurs in the mind first; mind is supreme and everything is permeated by mind only.)

XXX

32. Taking Offence To Innocuous Merry-making

Enter Protagonist

Of the many a memory that I cherish and retain is the camaraderie I enjoyed with my cousin who was bit older to me. By my perspective, he was not of perfectly sound mind; he suffered from stammering and stuttering speech and his mouth was ever salivating. He was sort of weak-brained. Otherwise also, his I Q seemed to be below normal even as a child. We children were allowed to play together but not to venture beyond the bounds of the homesteads. Houses actually in those days were not like those of these days; those were *kutcha* habitats with lot of precincts which were outstretched beyond the roofed area. We played at an elevated open platform near the house.

The children had their tantrums and they kept on singing songs of odd types whatever came to their minds. I and my playmate as well used to indulge in merry-making of different sorts. And our parents, particularly, mothers were convinced that we were at ease in playing together.

One day, what happened that a storm of dust, followed by

dark clouds and thunder-storm, set off when we were out, playing. For such an occasions, we had one pet rhyme for chanting aloud, like as follows:

Aandhee aayee mehu aayau,
Badee bahoo kau jethu aayau!
(Dust storm has arrived and thunder-storm has struck too; it seems as though the elder brother of the husband of the eldest housewife has arrived!)

There was an apparent contradiction and irony in the childish rhyme.

I started chanting the same on seeing the storm coming, out of sheer joy. However, to my utter surprise and dismay, my playmate took offence to my rhyming this innocuous couplet. I could not fathom what was offending in that rhyme for my friend. He said, "Don't you chat that rhyme; it's against the dignity of my mother."

"How come it offends the dignity and respect of your mother?" I enquired quite baffled.

" 'Cause it's my mother who is the eldest housewife in this house."

"Nevertheless, I am not chanting with reference to your mother." I rejoindered.

"It matters little; yet it hurts my sentiments and those of my mother, that is, your elder aunt."

Still I kept on chanting, merry-making on the oncoming dust-storm. My playmate ran towards his mother, me in his footsteps, quite hopeful that he was in the wrong and I was in the right. My mother also overheard our petition to our elder aunt but opted to keep mum and away from the whole childish affair; she was actually almost the junior most housewife in the vast household of joint family and, incidentally, the petition was filed before the eldest lady whose writ ran in the household next, of course, only to the grand-ladies. Then only, for the first time, I realised that hierarchy might be so tyrannical as well and might stifle even the sane thinking and truth itself.

The eldest lady – my elder aunt -- ruled in his son's favour at length despite my pleading fervently in support of my innocuous views. To add fuel to fire, or salt to the wound, so to say, even the grandfather of the boy, as I can vividly recollect, rebuked me for such profane tongue as if it were against his daughter-in-law. I felt bad, even as, this was a foretaste of the rampant nepotism and lack of sensitivity and wisdom in the adults, in the society, and in the world at large.

What sort of a world it is! I may not mean to hurt the feelings of anybody, yet by implication, it might be taken as having hurt the feelings of somebody.

33. *Insensitive Grown-ups*

Enter Protagonist

I have received the WhatsApp message from my younger brother reading *'Modhoo Chaachaajee* is no more'. I felt compelled to exclaim in response: 'A nice fellow is gone!' followed by 'All must die ultimately!' *Modhoo Chaachaajee's* personality was defined succinctly by my brother in these words, 'He was the last icon or ancestor of our pedigree who was effective and influential amongst all members old and gen-next equally. He was well-versed with the genealogy, heritage and relationships of our clan. He exercised his clout even on the gen-next – a graceful clout, a respectful place amongst youth of the clan'.

And I get transported into another realm, back to my babyhood days when I was merely a toddler and set off reminiscing *Modhoo Chaachaajee* as a scary person who scared me away whenever he happened to meet me on the way whenever I ventured out of my house onto the lane of the village.

He used to rush towards me raising alarm as if there was a great danger -- for me – and resultantly, I rushed back in alarm towards my mother's lap ruing the misdemeanour of elders who did not care for the feelings of a baby or a child. In that state of babyhood as well, I can remember my feeling of antagonism towards such people in that they behaved savagely instead of treating a baby or a child with love and affection as well as caressing. A baby was aware how grown-ups ought to behave with the babies but those grown-ups were not aware! This was the standard of rearing of babies in that society I grew up in!

And *Modhoo Chaachaa* was not alone: whoever was grown-up – my father included – was in the despicable habit of mistreating the babies. My mother, of course, took cudgels with *Modhoo Chaachaa* and the like, and pointed out their follies to them but to no avail. Next time again the same savagery was at display whenever I tried to gain confidence by venturing out of my mother's lap.

A grave sort of diffidence has set in, as a result, in my psyche, and I have never been an extrovert and sociable person in my life!

Modhoo Chaachaa was not the only menace for the child that I was, there were other multifarious dangers galore in the rustic environs, like, one mad man of the village. He was of deranged mind and had special antipathy towards a phrase or word *'Drooch'* which had no meaning in itself. Whenever someone uttered this word -- unintelligible word, of course --

within the range of his hearing, he darted precariously against the person; and when he did so, he resembled a dreadful bull charging against another bull. Incidentally, there was no dearth of enraged bulls, as well, venting their ire against human species in the village alleys; however, those beasts did lose their temper only when someone might have hurt them without any cause. In that eventuality, if someone came in his way – of the deranged man -- if only innocently, one would get hurt; and the danger for the innocent babies and kids was all the more. We children dreaded this daemon of a creature in human shape more than anything else on the planet; for a soul without brain, or with a malfunctioning cerebrum, is the most dangerous entity thinkable. The same may be true for machines operated by artificial intelligence (the AI). This *Drooch*-man was quite an adult when we watched him. Fortunately for us, he died soon thereafter. God has designed sensibly an early death for fools and madcaps.

XXX

Table of Contents

34. Childish Defensive Misadventure

Enter Protagonist

In my babyhood, I have the impression that the race I was born into had the adults who drew sadistic pleasure from teasing and nagging the babies. My baby conscience suggested instead to me that the elders ought to behave affectionately towards babies and children. Unfortunately that was conspicuously absent a trait in the entire race I was born into. To walk out alone and face an adult on the way was akin to a cub facing a male lion. The adage that the progeny of a lioness have hordes of homicidal adversaries, starting with their own begetter, the reigning lion. *(Sher ke jaaye ko sau jokhey!)*

Our ancestors were supposedly a martial race and their progeny were by nature conditioned mentally in that ever recurrent mode of belligerence and misdemeanour! They were in all probability the progenies of the warriors of war of *Maraathaas* when the latter were on the winning spree in northern India.

On paternal side if *Modhoo Chaachaa* was a constant terror for me, on maternal side it was our maternal uncle, the cousin of my mother: *Mahendra Maamaa*, the same persona whose wife I had fetched from the nearby village mocking as her husband. What a coincidence! Both were *Mahendra* and both were addicted to teasing the babies and did draw sadistic pleasure in this diabolical pursuit. I used to curse both of them from the bottom of my heart repeatedly, but to no respite. I used to shower curses on my father, as well, for that matter, for he was equally tyrannical!

Once in my *Naanee*'s village I was sitting with other children of the same age at the sprawling ground of our *Naanaa's* male living place. Other elders were present, too. *Mahender Maamaa* was present, too, and I was apprehensive that *Maamaa* would berate and humiliate me to the exclusion of other kids -- of his own clan. It did happen exactly as per my apprehension! But I was not willing to take this humiliation lying down this time, filled with malice as my heart was at that moment. When he teased and troubled me, I reacted sharply, "I shall make you be beaten by my father; dare not visit my village!" I was serious in my intent since I had great faith in my father's superiority so far as ferocity towards fellow humans and especially us was concerned. I presumed that a ferocious person would be ferociously disposed towards one and all; but the reality is on the contrary: a ferocious man behaves affably with another ferocious man. He torments and troubles only the polite, simple and meek souls! As soon as I muttered these angry words with a menacing countenance beckoning to *Mahender Maamaa*, I became the butt of joke for everybody present there. They took my remark as a pleasurable charade by a little baby only!

Maamaa said mockingly to me, "Oh, then you will get us beaten by your father? Are we scared of your father? We aren't!"

Other elders including my mates started repeating what I had just uttered as a refrain, to tease me later on for weeks together: 'so he will evoke his father's wrath to set all of us right!'

Words, however genuine in intent, coming as they did from the mouth of a child, were taken but as a matter of farce and a material for merry-making for times to come. Also, it was then only that I realised that my father who behaved so rashly and harshly towards us family folks was not at all a scary personality for those elders, the outsiders!

What may be the remedy then? I was faced with this bigger poser. However, after this abnormal reaction from my side, I felt, that *Mahender Maamaa* had changed tack and, instead of scaring me like *Modhoo Chaachaa,* he now used to repeat my threat mockingly whenever I came across him.

XXX

35. My First Falls And Elderly Disdain

Enter Protagonist

Of the plethora of dim, foggy memories of my babyhood, one that haunts me still today is the following one.

My father being an anarchist, an irresponsible lad, an indolent youth, was used to sending his paraphernalia – his wife and his issues – to his in-laws too frequently, rather, (as was later explicitly expressed by one of the members of his in-laws), whenever he found himself without resources including even food and cereals for feeding himself and his family, he would -- as though it was his matrimonial privilege -- shift his share of responsibility towards his in-laws: under what clause of morality or clause of matrimony, I can't say.

He was the scion of a prestigious pedigree (probably linked to some royal lineage as suggested by hints thrown up by circumstances obtaining just preceding my coming of age and of senses); he possessed quite a chunk of arable land to his individual share (15 *beeghaas*, almost 5 acres) of very fertile soil; he had inherited quite a substantial amount of gold and silver from his paternal side, and also from his wife's sides; he had grabbed quite a fortune in the name of dowry from his in-laws (since dowry in those days was a prestigious tradition, the more the better); he was an exceptionally advanced educated person of his area (the only person who had graduated in his time as I was made

to believe, right or wrong!); he had connections with high and mighty of his time, courtesy of his father's stature and friendships with big officers of all hues even during British *Raaj, et al.*

Still to no avail! Not at all a worthy soul!

He could not afford even two morsels of food either for himself or for his not-so-small family. Not only this, he floundered everything he possessed: the prestige of the family (he did not feel any qualms of conscience or shame on begging money or *Beedee* - - tobacco leafy pipe -- from any Tom, Dick and Harry); the land (which he never cultivated, rather, that was ever a liability for us, a burden); the gold (he sold off even his baby son's gold bangles when the latter was a toddler, and squandered it off – he was such an unemotional fiend! Whenever my mother narrated to me this incident she always sighed woefully and tears flooded her eyes!); and silver (the last bulk of the half kg of which he obliged my aged maternal grandfather – *Naanaajee* -- to give him to save the land from the clutches of money-lenders in whose stranglehold he ever loved to remain!); education he could not complete – so much so that even as simple and inconsequential a degree as that of B. Ed. he could not procure – because he was a loafer having come in the company of his feudal relatives, and also, he never thought it expedient to complete the B. Ed. for securing his career later on, he was such an educated duffer, even as, he depended on his and his father's connections for his livelihood, yet he never pursued anything to the logical conclusion (this I am saying after hearing him umpteen number of times whereby he would narrate his tales of woe, in which he could be caught lacking common-sense and logical conclusion); land – the last bastion of family's prestige – he sold off a couple of years before his prolonged as well as belated death under duress from his middle son who was a carbon copy of himself in truest sense, (and the 'worthy' son frittered away even the last paisa of sale proceeds on liquor served to his roguish accomplices) *et al.*

In these woeful as well as heart-rending circumstances, my mother who was from a prestigious, sensible and industrious family was obliged to lead her married life!

My elder maternal uncle used to come to my father's village quite frequently, or at times, he made it to *Cholaa* Rly. Stn. unto which my father would take his family and from there the maternal uncle – who was a fiery personality, not an affectionate personality -- would take us by passenger train to *Daanwar* Rly. Stn, hardly two stations in between. I have a feeling that I feared trains under the misgiving that it was mechanical and would not heed the command of human beings, or would start moving while entraining, thus dropping the passengers off.

Normally, the timings of these trains were such that we had to leave the abode quite early in the morning and had to do journey in the dark. This riddle I could never resolve; this was possibly with the idea that my maternal uncle, unlike my father, would not like to waste his day: he loved to do labour in the fields the whole day.

One instance of early hour journey (from the perspective of a baby/ a child) I am recalling that has stuck to my psyche; so bruising it was! After travelling in the passenger train from *Cholaa* to *Daanwar*, we alighted at *Daanwar* in the wee hours, or I thought these were wee hours: the dawn. I got conscious only on alighting at the station platform. I might have been asleep during the journey.

I was merry at the idea of going to my *Nansaar*, the abode of my maternal grandmother. Going to *Nansaar* always filled me with tremendous amount of pleasure: it was so pleasing to be at *Nansaar*! On the contrary, it was so gloomy at the village of my father! On *Nansaar* side, there was greenery, feeling of well-being, atmosphere of mirth and civility, commitment for corporeal labour etc, whereas on the side of father and grandfather's village, it was a tense atmosphere (due to the daemonic presence of my father: he was never an affable figure in my memory, all the more torturing in my babyhood psyche. I always longed for his absence from the scene.), *sans* any plants and trees, confinement to the small limit of small, *kutcha*, thatched house, with no room for physical labour at all. The men on the side of my father did not believe in physical (or even mental labour, feudalistic as they were), nor did they believe in the freedom for womenfolk. On the side of our maternal grandmother, it was freedom for womenfolk, and also, they were supposed to work in the fields. That kept them busy instead of always thinking something filthy and fishy due to inactivity. I liked that sort of busy life-style. I think, that way both the sides were way apart culturally as well as conceptually.

Ironically, my fatherly side people claimed themselves to be more civilised (*baareek* as they called that specific attribute of theirs), whereas my motherly side people called my fatherly side people as worthless indolent fellows. In my perception, the motherly side were more judicious. On fatherly side, people were carved in stone what they called tradition,

which was nothing but foolhardiness and skulduggery at the most!

Our *Nansaar* was a few miles afar, along the railways. We set off for the *Nansaar*: *Maamaajee* in the lead, I beckoned by my mother to follow *Maamaajee*, then my mother with a baby on her lap to the rear. By that time, only that was the size of my father's crop (albeit, later on, it prospered to huge proportions, un-feedable as well as unaffordable proportions).

What we were treading was the gravel path along the railway line, criss-crossed also by the telephone wires and several metallic poles of different heights. I being a baby was unsuspecting of the riskiness of such impediments. I started walking like I was walking on a plane surface, like in my level surfaced house. The result was that I stumbled. *Maamaajee* looked back, mother hurried off to lift me and *Maamaajee* didn't say anything, that being my first instance of fall: that grace mark he gave me. Mother warned me to be more careful while treading the unsteady gravel path; her tone was mixed with some anguish perhaps due to the feeling that next time if I fell, her brother would burst out, not only on her baby but also on her.

But a baby is a baby after all: only after stepping a few feet I again stumbled. I could not make out why I was stumbling, that was a great conundrum for me as well at that tender age. This time, both *Maamaajee* and my mother growled, and reprimanded me, "Walk carefully! Why can't you walk carefully? *Eh?*" I could not understand why they were flogging me instead of being sympathetic towards me, a baby, having got hurt by fall on an unsteady and gravelled path! The difference of perceptions of a baby and an adult! I longed for being lifted onto the lap of my mother: by that age possibly I had been used to being on the lap of my mother; the baby on the lap of my mother was, I suppose, my brother (who later on died in babyhood itself).

In the process, I fell many a time (despite the pejorative language used by my *Maamaajee* and the ensuing embarrassment of my mother due to the annoyance displayed each time by my *Maamaajee*). I being a baby, however, could find no fault with myself for my frequent downfalls: it was all the fault of my mother who was not taking me on to her lap!

Anyway, slowly and steadily, with my tender age and body being the cause of slow movement from station to *nansaar*, we reached *nansaar*. I was so glad to have reached the Elysium of my fancies. It was morning hours. And the season was winter (because bonfires were on by that time).

I quickly changed into domestic casuals from the travel's artificial showy attire and, as if to show off something to *Maamaajee* and other village folk, rushed towards the bonfire that was being burned outside. I was under the impression and harboured the perception that I being a baby and quite grown up by that time and being their sister's son would be treated with exceptional love and affability.

On the contrary!

As soon as I reached the spot of bonfire, my *Maamaajee* and yet another person of his ilk and age, instead of greeting and welcoming me, derided me, *Maamaajee* divulging to his fellow, "Lo, here is the scion of *Barhwaalaas* (this was the appellation or denomination of my paternal grandfatherly family), you know, he fell half a dozen times on the way, such a strong-bodied boy he is!" Whole of my enthusiasm of having come to *nansaar* was evaporated. Not only this, whole of my regard for those elderly duo was gone, too. I felt something broken in my interior psychically. Still I maintained facade and tried to smile (to protect my fragile baby psyche). But the humiliating behaviour of those insensitive people continued at the cost of my psyche and self-esteem. And I left the scene.

How deeply it had hurt me can be gauged by the fact that still today, after six odd decades I have been obliged to narrate the finer details of that unsavoury episode. This also shows how the adults are insensitive towards the feelings of the babies and the children. I developed an enduring disdain forever in my heart towards such insensitive adults. In what respect are they adults, or any different from babies or children -- all the same!

XXX

36. Fall From The Well-Head

Enter Protagonist

This memory dates back to the period when I was not even conscious of my existence, what to speak of social relations and the hurts and risks involved therein. In our village in the ground of our family's residences there was a well of potable water. This well was used not only for fetching drinking water for all the households of our closely-knit family but also served as the source of water for all other purposes whatsoever. People took their bath on the well only – diving in the attached pond; we too.

One day my elder uncle (*Taujee*) was taking bath at the periphery around the well, that is, at the well-head. I felt tempted to take a bath, too. It might have been summer days. I climbed up the slippery pucca periphery of the well and reached beside the uncle. He poured bucketful of water on my head, to my amusement and pleasure. And thereafter he instructed me to unwet and dry myself standing on the boundary of the well.

And lo! I slipped from the slippery and wet boundary of the well-head onto the rugged and jutted ground beside the well strewn with stones, pebbles and rocks. My skull got opened with blood oozing out. At this moment I can't remember whether I was feeling any pain or not, that is why I said that I was of the age when I didn't know how to feel pain or how to relish pleasure. I was beyond the pale of pain and pleasure! I might have become unconscious quite possibly, that's why I could not recall the feeling of pain.

But the later developments and the sombre mood of the entire family, especially of my loving mother, revealed to me that something unusual had happened to me. Some primary treatment was given by applying turmeric powder to the opening in the skull, and later on I had to do piggyback riding on my father's back to and fro the nearby town for regular dressing of the skull for weeks together. The *Jarraah* (sort of rustic surgeon) who seemed to be faithful to my father, and also, to the humanity – despite he being a *Muslim* and I being a *Hindoo* – treated my open skull deftly; and after probably a few months, the wound got filled as well as cured, but a big scar is still there ever present on my skull, big enough to remind me of that *karma-phal* (fallout of some sin done previously).

I have a hunch that it is because of this almost fatal fall from the slippery well-head that resulted in opening of my skull that my brain has become extraordinarily sharp as though not the skull but the doors of intelligence and wisdom were opened with the opening of *khopadee* (skull)! Oftentimes calamity stalks as a boon in disguise!

XXX

37. Mischief With The Aunt At The Well-head

Enter Protagonist

Aside from the skull opening mishap at the well-head I have a few pleasant memories as well concerning that. On the same periphery of the family well, we toddlers used to be taken for bath by our youngest aunt – *Buaa* -- that is, the youngest sister of my father. She was a simpleton as her mother had died leaving her only an infant as I have delineated in the case of my father hereinbefore. She lacked emotional quotient as do the children who lose their parents in babyhood and are deprived of the motherly affection and hugs.

I can recall at least one such instance wherein I and my two cousins were taking bath at the well's periphery – the well-head -- being commanded as well as controlled by our the then adolescent aunt. We were toddlers yet but we were aware that it was a great pleasure to make mischief so as to tease our *Buaajee* who was herself only an adolescent girl at that time. The aunt would rebuke all the three of us in mock annoyance and displeasure; and even threatened us with dire consequences should we continue with our tantrums. Her insincere displeasure rather added to our childish mirth, and we indulged in varieties of mischief-making in its wake.

But, I feel in the hindsight, that after the incident of fall from the well-head, I was most likely prohibited from going to the well to avoid any repeat of such a mishap. My mother was displeased, rather suspicious, that I being a child was not taken proper care of by my elder uncle at the well head and that the latter might have deliberately let me fall down so that I – his nephew – might die, and the entire worth of the household would go to his own heirs, sons. The human society and psyche was sort of this type of thinking and mores; not a very noble minded society!

XXX

38. Khwaahum-khwaa *(Senseless Charade)*

Enter Grandfather

On the sloping ascent to our high-rise male residences, which we called *khedaa,* there are two toddlers of hardly 3 years of age each, both cousins, wallowing in the dry as well as fine dust of the slanted gravel path. The slopy path has for last few days been beaten to very fine dust by traversing feet of inhabitants and visitors on it. These small toddlers can think of no better material on earth than this dried fine dust-powder. They have smeared their whole bodies with white dust – just like having applied talcum powder. Also, they are throwing the fistfuls of dust powder into the sky.

To this merry-making of theirs, my elder brother, who otherwise is very short-tempered, reacts naught, to my surprise. I pass by these kids to climb the *khedaa* and lo, they throw the dust on to me as well and give a loud laugh as if it was the greatest pleasure of their lives. And mine, too!

"Why are you raising dust and making so much noise *khwaahum-khwaa?"* I shouted in mock disgust and displeasure.

"Why are you raising dust and making so much noise *khwaahum-khwaa!",* prompt came the reciprocating as well as echoing chorus of both the boys deriding me, *"Khwaahum-khwaa! Khwaahum-khwaa!"* They started chanting in unison, in chorus.

I and my elder brother exchanged chuckles, even as, overtly exhibiting vexation at this rout.

"What is *khwaahum-khwaa?* What is *khwaahum-khwaa?",* they started asking me in a commanding tone. I could not make out whether they were asking me question, that is, the meaning of *khwaahum-khwaa* or just deriding me to indicate that there was nothing in the world which could be termed as irrelevant or as meaningless. If anything is meaningless or purposeless, then everything whatsoever on this planet is meaningless only, for that matter. The latter perception might be my mature and educated mind's outcome, as the children could not be that sharp as to think like this, so I offered to define the word *'khwaahum-khwaa'* to both of them.

"Khwaahum-khwaa means senseless, without any purpose, behaving wastefully, meaninglessly, in a naughty manner! Why are you doing this dirty merry-making which has no use and does not behove you gentle chaps?" I tried to preach them as if they were some intelligible school-going students.

But they were kids and their only aim was to make merry by any trick whatsoever and at whosoever's cost. They kept on chanting the same phrase or refrain. We elders got amused though. My elder brother clarified that for the kids this word was quite new and quite worth playing with!

So, they kept on playing with *'Khwaahum-khwaa'* nonchalantly! Playing with the words was a new discovery for them! Only sensible words or phrases which we comprehend are worth recognising, all the rest which we can't comprehend are amusing only, even for grown-ups.

One of these two kids was my grandson, the son of my arguably deranged son.

The episode would have ended there but for my youngest daughter, the same motherless child, who happened to pass by at the material time and was witness to this mirthful childish activity of the two kids. She caught hold of my grandson, shouted at him mockingly, reprimanding him for his temerity to deride an old man, that too, his grandfather. Then she took him by arm to the ladies' residences. There she was overheard narrating the entire dusty tale to the toddler's mother and others with additional inputs from her side, like, 'he was deriding my father by asking him the meaning of *khwaahum-khwaa*, and that he continued to tease his grandfather for quite a while. How audacious he is! How intelligent or inquisitive he is!', she exclaimed laughingly,

enjoying the childish feats, the mother Nature's spontaneous and innocent source of happiness.

XXX

39. Wall Shall Crumble, Kids!

Enter Protagonist

In those days of timelessness and sense of eternity in our life during babyhood, I noticed an old man – who later came out to be identified as my real grandfather. He used to interfere with our childish revelry: for valid reasons, at that, now I realise. But at the time he forbade us from playing at certain places we felt intense irritation and antagonism towards him.

One such spot used to be a *kutcha* wall which now I suppose was in a dilapidated state of repair. But we kids did not have an idea about the collapse of a wall, or about getting trapped under its debris, or least of all, about our dying as a fall-out of the collapse of a ramshackle wall. The wall in its rickety state sort of represented the woebegone state of the lineage itself of this one time high and mightily grand family. The entire pedigree was on downward slide. Still they were sticking to their hollow arrogance, conceit and prestige.

Grandpa used to come rushing and rebuking us all whenever he saw us playing beside or beneath that dilapidated wall. He would pronounce to one and all that the wall was about to fall and, as a result, we were about to die. We were, however, ourselves little concerned whether we died or survived as a fallout of the collapse of the wall in question. We being children had a birth right to upbraid our grandpa in return for his alacrity in disturbing our game, in which, we used to be so deeply engrossed. We wondered why grandpa ought to be more worried about our well-being and life than we ourselves were!

XXX

40. Dust-Storm And Grandpa's Shouts Of Alarm

Enter Protagonist

Not only us little children, even the housewives were bemused at grandpa's obsessive compulsive disorder (OCD) concerning the prospect of break out of bonfire in the wake of a sudden dust-storm in the village. Whenever there was the onslaught of a dust-storm or thunder-storm on the hamlet – and the frequency of such incidents was quite high during dry days of the summer season – the grandpa was seen rushing hither and thither – almost knocking at the door of every which household – forewarning the assumingly ignorant housewives that the latter ought to extinguish fire in the family hearth lest the spark from the oven should result in an inferno and gut the entire hamlet. The ladies generally obliged, yet majority of them were amused at *Baabaa*'s OCD.

Our *Baabaa*'s precocious approach, or so to say, the over cautiousness was owing to the fact that all the homesteads at that time in our hamlet were thatched houses, meaning thereby, built of turf and dried grass etc; hardly any pucca house was found in those days. And a thatch and fire are old time lovers; or enemies!

Grandpa was the only educated person, not only in the hamlet but in the entire surrounding area. As a result of school education, due to development of bookish intellect and analytical power, his sense of risk in every aspect of life, especially, social life had been aggravated excessively. The happenings that aroused little alarm in the minds of other villagers or house-holds aroused terrible sense of alarm in the mind of our grandpa.

Like a baby does not dread anything, even a venomous snake or burning fire, yet a snake and fire are fatal and ferocious, the assessment of *Baabaajee* was correct and that of others innocent, ignorant or negligent without doubt. Innocence or negligence may not safeguard one's interests. One has to be aware of the reality including the risks involved in every phenomenon, every aspect of living process: whether it be in the realm of Nature, or relating to society, or concerning one's or others' lives!

XXX

11. Lure Of Cinema

Enter Protagonist

Of that fanciful and pampered babyhood, I can recall one more interesting instance when one fine day I found myself busy playing with other kids of my age in my *Nanihaal*. My sweet memories are mostly related to my stay at *Nanihaal* only. After a while, I noticed that my mother was not being seen around for quite a long time – maybe, for days together – and I got anxious; for a baby one's mother is the quintessential entity and that was missing from the scene. How was I oblivious to the fact of my dear mother's absence for such a long time was attributable to the fact that in *Nanihaal*, I was favourite of everybody, particularly of my *Naanee* and I was her great fan, too. She was so affectionate! When my *Naanee* was around I felt no alarm at the unusual absence of my mother from the normal scene of life.

Then at length I started feeling alarmed and started asking my *Naanee* and others, "Where is my *Beebee*?" I addressed my mother by the appellation of *Beebee* – which was the synonym of sister in colloquial parlance and since I noticed her elder or younger brothers call her '*Beebee*', I picked up that appellation and started addressing her by this word, too. My *Naanee* being an affable personality tried to assuage me by making other kids play with me and by offering sweets etc. But finally my patience gave way and I started making a scene of it all: 'Where is my *Beebee*? Where is my *Beebee*?'

Incidentally, the day I breached the limit of patience was the day of my mother's return from the town where she had been to on some secret expedition, accompanying her sister-in-law, that is, the wife of my younger *Maamaajee*.

Naanee took us kids to the railway track which was beside our *Nanihaal* and by that time it was simply a single track: I am talking of those days! Reaching the track, we noticed that the highway for laying the double track was being prepared and it was quite a pleasure to run on the high road laid for the second railway track. The frequency of trains – both passenger and goods – was very low those days; so there was very little risk of being crushed or cut by the trains; for the timings of trains were almost certain and known to everybody like the back of the palms of one's hands. We started playing on that mud road and went quite afar. It was *Naglaa Kath* and we were running towards *Daanwar* railway station. At the back of my mind I had my mother who was conspicuous by her absence, yet the presence of my *Naanee* was filling that void and keeping my anxiety at bay. *Naanee* had a great gift for lulling the babies and loved them quite a lot.

After sometime, we saw silhouettes of three persons, looming along the track from the side of the railway station. Seeing them coming, the other babies accompanying me beckoned to me pointing towards them: 'Your mother is coming.' I felt all at once so glad: my mother was coming! The trio approached us and they consisted of my mother, my *Maamee* and my maternal cousin – elder *Daadaa*. My mother embraced me resembling a cow, as though I was her forlorn calf.

The kids started teasing me telling that my mother had gone to the town for watching cinema and had not taken me along with her, thereby depriving me of the entertainment. I started believing the charade and tried to make a scene before my mother and *Maamee*. However, they assuaged me that it was all humbug what my playmates were uttering: they were simply teasing me to rouse me against my mother.

But that episode of my mother having left me back and allegedly having watched the cinema alone along with her *Bhaabhee* stuck into my psyche as if I had been deprived of some great

opportunity, of some great boon. Nonetheless, now I feel that watching of cinema was beyond the pale of baby's psyche and it fitted only the mental build of the adults as well as grown-ups. For a deal of lust, sex and glamour is at display there in the cinemas; it was true even then, it is true even these days.

XXX

42. Origins Of Depravity & Dissipation

Enter Protagonist

The creation as well as consciousness of the cosmos is closely related to the phenomenon of sexual activity: it's rather a constant flow of sexual intercourses. Entire nature is manifestly a proof of this ubiquitous phenomenon. Human beings are not exception to that, too.

Whereas all such innocuous and innocent activities of babyhood or childhood did continue, associated with all sorts of feelings, sentiments and emotions, there was another undercurrent too, that was not so un-perturbing. We kids might be innocent and unaware of such evils but the society abounds in such evil spirits as well, who indulge in such profane and depraved actions, and also, ensnare others in their activities. There is no escaping such loops.

Once a person who was somewhat elder to us asked us kids

to accompany him to his agricultural fields – sugarcane fields to be precise – where he promised us to give sugarcane. We children – how could we suspect his depravity, we were quite ignorant about such activities or misdeeds -- we accompanied him to his fields. He made all others to stay at the edge of the field and took one of our playmates inside the field. We did not understand anything of this game or machination on his part. After sometime, the playmate came out, even as, we could not discern any change in his complexion or countenance, nor could he himself; of course, he was holding a sugarcane in his hand and was satisfied. Then he took another child inside and the same story got repeated. The same thing happened with me as well. At last he took my elder cousin inside and the latter came back unusually sooner and fretting and fuming. He divulged the depravity of the scoundrel who had seduced us all children. My cousin told us that the scoundrel had been fucking us kids inside the sugarcane field, ignorant as we were, not knowing the name of the obscene and despicable game. When we denied the charge, my cousin enquired if the scoundrel had stripped us and made us to sit on his lap and did embrace us. We nodded in affirmation and he declared that all of us had been fucked and defiled

by the dissipated person, and that the person was a paedophile. Despite so much scene created by our cousin we could not fathom ABC of this ugly episode or phenomenon of depravity.

Nonetheless, we observed that the scoundrel did not come out of the field and had fled from the scene from the farther side of the sugarcane field. Now, the question arose: how could we escape such ensnarement on the part of depraved elders? Ignorance is a great weakness and leads to exploitation and defilement, even rapes in later life. I feel, there is need for apprising the gullible children of such depravity in clear terms so that they can guard themselves against such inducements of elders.

Almost the similar instances happened when we children took bath in the brook near our village. Its depth was not much; it was merely to cover the ankles or upto knees. In that water when we played, some of our playmates who were somewhat elder to us tried to fuck us and we were completely unaware of the depravity of the act: we thought that the action was very interesting as well as amusing. Once incidentally when our elders caught sight of us indulged in such depravity, they beat us and then did we realise that something obscene was being played on our innocent carnal child bodies. Children are thus innocent preys of elders' sexual lust! The cosmos is after all the constant flow of sexual intercourses! Apart from the social stream, the political stream, the financial stream, the academic stream of life, there is also a sexual stream of life that runs covertly deep inside all these overt streams and affects all the other aspects of life: social, familial, financial, political *et al.* This aspect affects the whole scenario indirectly yet definitely very strongly. And people normally do not come to know of this undercurrent when it comes to deciding the factors behind some incident occurring.

At *Naanee*'s village as well, when my maternal uncle's son and I used to sleep together, he was in the habit of fondling with my sex organ, even as, I disliked it badly and felt irritated; but due to fear of elders coming to know, I did not shout and let him continue with this depravity. In later life, this activity developed into a bad habit of masturbation with me which I never could overcome, to be very true. In later life, this origin of depravity could not be recalled; but at this moment, I can well recollect and connect that bad habit to the sleeping together of an innocent guy with a bad guy.

The children should not be left at the mercy of other elders or even other children of the same age group unobserved or without watch at least. The undercurrent of sexual activities is so hideous, yet ironically it is neglected totally in all the considerations and decisions of life and society!

XXX

43. Erstwhile Regality Decimated By Legality

Enter Protagonist

Life does not leave its indelible traces on the gravelled dust-way of memory in respect of every single incident; only the saddest and the merriest happenings get recorded in the black-box of memory. While reconstructing my babyhood I am forgetting many an event of prime significance. Those crop up when I stop thinking about or think about closing this province of my life's landscape which is beyond the pale of time and space. During this particular period it was immaterial as well as impossible for me the babe to ascertain which time it was or which place it was where all these episodes took place, or occurred of their own. Time and space did make their entry in my life's journey only in the next phase.

While narrating the sweet memory of attending the wedding party of the son of my maternal uncle — *bhaaisaahab* -- I have inadvertently omitted the *Gaunaa* ceremony connected therewith wherein, too, I participated. After a few months, the *Gaunaa* was arranged and my maternal uncle – the younger one -- along with one or two more close relatives went to the same place where the marriage had taken place; and I was taken as a child to accompany them, which was felt necessary so as to communicate with the newly wed young bride. Bride is veiled and can't communicate with elders of the family, thus only an innocent child is used as a medium to communicate with that mute cattle of a female soul!

In my vivid memory, still I can recollect the special recognition afforded to me by the hosts at that village, the reason being that I was related to the most influential persona and family of that village. When my caretakers informed the hosts that I was a scion of *badhwaalaas* and was related to so and so in that village, they immediately got overawed by my presence: they started treating me with special adoration which was quite heady a feeling for me, a child. How lucky I was those days! To be born to such influential and well-to-do relatives, having big name and fame!

This big relative of ours was but the husband of my grandfather's elder sister, and he was the landlord of the area, also, sort of a warlord, a mafia, if you would like to call them.

Here, I hasten to add that the impression of greatness lasted only in my child memory's background, since on attaining adulthood, I found no more that influence nor the clout of that family in their area; the departure of Britishers had had its ill effect on the erstwhile aristocracy and the landed gentry. In lieu thereof, new aristocracy was taking roots which was hitherto quite subjugated to those erstwhile influential people. The new Constitution was framed keeping in mind the interests of new breed of politicians and lawyers and to the decimation of the erstwhile clan of politicians – the feudal fiefdoms, princely states, warlords and landlords -- who were conventionally christened as royalty. The framing of the new Constitution of *Bhaarat* predominantly by lawyers, educated in English Law, proved lethal for the erstwhile gentry and cost them their everything. Their everything was snatched away and shattered! This was a game played by the new breed of power brokers in connivance with the fleeing rulers on the old breed of power brokers!

XXX

44. Kuldevee & Kuldevataas & Underlying Logic
Enter Protagonist

Yet another memory is

concerning our garden, our orchard, which was a few furlongs afar from the hamlet. This garden or orchard abounded in multiple species of trees and plants bearing fruits of different types: mangoes, guavas, jambolan (*syzygium cumini*), lemon, even bananas (that were required for making *mandap* – pavilion -- for wedding ceremonies), *neem*, mulberry, fig *et al*. More than for the fruits, the garden was a matter of fondness because of its soothing shades and greenery and vegetation. It gave a sense of collectivity, a miniature array or museum of entire Nature's miracles. Like all other phenomena of the universe, this orchard was also ever changing; in every season or even every month, its complexion was found different. People took rest and saved themselves from the heat and scorching sun by taking shelter under their shades. For us children, this garden represented the whole cosmos -- full of all sorts of miracles, both botanical as well as zoological.

In this family orchard, there were the graves of our dead ancestors, too – the word 'grave' is not proper since our ancestors were not buried there, rather, they used to be cremated in this garden; and presently, in lieu of graves, there were mausoleums sort of structures of make-shift type, under various trees – at their roots. Merely symbolical! These memorials were very funny indeed, now I think in hindsight. Some of them were well constructed, some were simply the assemblage of a few pucca bricks and quite a lot of them were simply one or two bricks kept under disparate trees for disparate ancestors. On the festive occasions of *Deewaalee* and *Holee*, we children along with the elders – ladies particularly – would visit these memorials and paid homage to the departed souls by offering cakes made of cow-dung or lighting clay lamps there. We also offered sweets on certain festivals there. That sort of *karm-kaand* was really enthralling: we never thought that those brickbats were nothing but the excuses for arousing veneration for our ancestors and for remembering them on this pretext or the other. What a wonderful tradition it was indeed! Our deceased ones ought to be remembered to draw inspiration from their lives lived in their times.

However queer or superstitious it might sound, I find substantial significance in this tradition, too; the life cannot be lived on mere dry logic; the psyche demands lots of fabricated fancies to keep itself sound and sane, and also, to fulfil the requirements of achieving a purpose.

In the same garden were there established our family gods and goddesses whatever. Of course, when deceased elders as well as ancestors were there, the gods and goddesses were bound to be found there only, amidst them only. Otherwise too, the *devataas* take the trees as their abode or vehicle – *vaahan,* it is told.

One such prominent – rather most dominant – goddess was the *Sheetalaa Maataa* who was venerated and worshipped on all the functions by and large. She was supposed to be taking care of the health-related issues of the children and adults, as well. If some child suffered from small-pox or measles, it was a sure shot sign of the wrath of *Sheetalaa Maataa*. Immediately the *Maataa* had got to be propitiated by offering songs in her praise by the hordes of family ladies. Those songs were *de facto* full of healing qualities: their vibrations had the effect of healing the sick person's soul and psyche and, in turn, the sick body. What a wonderful and amazing arrangement for healing!

XXX

45. *Dog-bites Along With Sugarcanes*

Enter Protagonist

As a toddler and babe I was a timid and shy creature, no doubt; I seldom ventured out of my parents' homestead. I recollect a day when my mother encouraged me to go into the village alley and see for myself how it felt like outside in the village.

The feeling inside the house is quite different from the feeling one gets while facing the outside world or in the alleys of hamlets and towns.

Striding slowly and steadily – hardly half a furlong away from my abode – I reached a nearby dwelling place of a relative of our family – in a village everybody is related and is treated as a family-member only, for that matter. This house had a huge banyan tree under whose shade were constructed two *kutcha* rooms, and all the rest was but a sprawling open space, rather a field – a *maidaan,* in which, the village children used to play and wrestle, or the village ladies used to defecate in the darkness of night. Those days, there was a sugarcane *Kolhoo* (crusher) installed in that *maidaan* and a great deal of activity kept on going on there concerning extraction of sugarcane juice and formation of jaggery and fine sugar from that by boiling in the huge cauldrons upon very large hearths.

Naturally, the sugarcanes were seen piled up there aplenty. That was a thing of attraction for children: they used to make away with sugarcanes stealthily. Nevertheless, I never indulged in such activities, shy and timid as I was by nature. However, that day I reached there, without any intention of getting sugarcanes or anything else whatsoever; simply following the commands of my mother to go on an outing. Incidentally, some ladies were perched there and the crusher activity was suspended, not going on at that particular moment. The adult ladies and their youngsters caught sight of me, and taking pity on me, as if I had gone there for fetching sugarcanes, they summoned me and asked if I wanted sugarcanes, to which, I replied in negative, and indeed it was so, I was sincere. But the ladies could not help taking pity on me and took me by arm and picked two or three sugarcanes from the pile and put the same on my shoulders. I felt bewildered and refused to take them because my mother did not permit of such activities, that is, accepting things from others. But the ladies insisted and loaded me with their unbidden bounty.

Somewhere in my heart I felt elated on having procured this bounty without asking and began to stride back towards my homestead. Hardly had I stepped ten or twelve feet that a dog barked upon me and rushed to bite, and bit me on the thigh, because my thigh was not very high at that age and the dog could easily take a mouthful of flesh from there. Bewildered, I dropped the sugarcanes and fell down crying piteously and morosely. I had this first tryst with dog-bite and menace of dogs. Menace of humans I could over hear quite aplenty from the mouths of all and sundry. Then I

realised for the first time: it's not safe to move on a path carrying something looking like a stick; the dogs and cattle would take offence to that, and would bite or hurt. In the later life, I also realised: it is not safe to move on the paths carrying anything valuable or beautiful; the anti-social elements would loot the valuables or rape the beauty. The real world is queer like that. Unintentionally too one can be an object of offence towards someone – it makes little difference whether one is human or beastly!

The episode was quite disheartening: I had been bitten by dog and was now susceptible to rabies. The zeal of getting sugarcanes was gone: to hell with sugarcanes and ladies, I mused. Concomitant to this dog-bite there was another dreadful prospect at home, that of rebuke by my mother and in the evening by my inconsiderate and intemperate father who would bark like dogs only. Why at all I ventured out, I thought; I should have kept myself confined to my room only, to remain safe and secure. But is that possible! One has to taste one's *karm-phalas* after all!

Later on, though, my father did not create a scene and was comparatively less insensible, both towards me and towards my mother: he did not beat my mother for this mishap and for allowing me to venture out. He, incidentally, never allowed his wife to venture out of the bounds of his homestead; she was treated like a tamed as well as tortured cattle. My father seemed to be dead sure that had my mother stepped out of her prison or pigeon-hole – the homestead -- the rapists would rape her and outrage her modesty and tarnish my father's prestige for good!

As an antidote to rabies, in our village, a family was known to be possessing the mystical powers or skills to administer a herbal drink – a concoction -- which was supposed to prevent any ill effects of dog-bite, the rabies, to be precise. Not only me but the entire clan of our family was administered the extremely obnoxious liquid in the wake of this dog-bite, and that resulted in nauseating vomiting by all and sundry, even as, it was semi-poisonous. The faith in this folk treatment was so deep that after intake of this drug we couldn't even suspect that rabies might afflict me ever in later life. *Vishasya Visham Aushadham!* (Remedy for poison is poison itself!)

XXX

46. Sugarcane And Human Heart vs Dog-bites

Enter Protagonist

The foregoing anecdote might give the impression that it's only dogs that bite following a misunderstanding about sugarcanes as sticks. That episode occurred at my paternal side of life. Here is another story on the maternal side, as well, to entirely contrary effect and implications. Almost at the same age I happened to be in my *Naanee*'s village, the season being that of winter and, consequently, conducive for crushing of sugarcanes once again. There was a *Kolhoo* – a crusher -- here as well, and it was also quite in the vicinity of our *Naanaa*'s residences. The stockpiles of sugarcanes were seen aplenty almost everywhere in the grounds.

One noontime, out of weariness, I thought of loitering around towards the *Kolhoo*, of my own volition this time. My maternal grandfather being a well-to-do and influential personage of the area I thought that it was my privilege to pick sugarcanes nonchalantly from the *Kolhoo,* and that nobody would object to or ought to object to that action of mine, even as, I was a guest of honour for the village: the son of one of their young ladies from the village. Without caring for the presence of the adults there I strode towards the piles of sugarcanes and picked up two good quality long sugarcanes and put them on my little shoulders, and started moving homeward as an indefatigable hero.

Hardly had I moved a few

96

steps from the spot of sugarcane pile that the owners of the sugarcane crop pounced upon me like hounds and barked upon me more precariously than the dogs in my village had done; I had a feeling just like that when those dogs bit me at the crusher in my village. They not only pitilessly rebuked me, but also, snatched away the sugarcanes from my hands. I was stunned at getting this unbecoming treatment from the human dogs who in the garb of adult humans were behaving worse than the dogs towards an innocent kid fondly enjoying possession of two sweet sticks which the mother Nature has endowed with sweetness. The same mother Nature has filled the adult human hearts with uttermost meanness, sourness and bitterness. I thought at that small age, as well, that their misdemeanour at any rate was unbecoming of grown-ups; they were insensitive beasts only in the form of human body. What could I do, except for crying and rushing to the rescue of my grandmother, that is, *Naanee*, who happened to be incidentally passing by at that moment, at that spot. She caught sight of me crying and being humiliated by those beastly canegrowers. She argued with them and chastised them for their meanness, and also proclaimed that their heart was meaner than that of a small child, and that there was no

difference between a small child and an adult like them in the absence of pathos and empathy towards small creatures. They disputed *Naanee*'s arguments, as well, that in that manner all their sugarcane crop would be taken away by people. My elder *Maamaajee* who was otherwise so ferocious also chastised them. Even at the cost of humiliation my *Naanee* grabbed one sugarcane for me somehow. But I didn't like the taste of sugarcane thereafter. Somewhere in my psyche I deduced that mean-minded people did not pay due respect to our maternal relatives too. That they could wrangle with them too. That was akin to crashing of a safety wall from the child's psyche. It's not expedient to enter into an argument or fight with a creature of mean mentality lacking self-esteem – be it human or animal or a beast!

Thereafter, I took a firm pledge that I should never ever pick anything from anybody's barn, leave alone the sugarcanes, for the rest of my life. And I lived upto my words throughout, and I have never even seen towards sugarcane piles thereafter throughout my life. I had realised that there was no major difference between dogs and human beings when it came to parting with a few sweet sticks of sugarcanes for the fancy of a kid. In the earlier episode, the owners had forcibly given me sugarcanes but the dogs bit my hips, whereas in the latter episode, I myself craved sugarcanes but the owners bit my innocent heart ruthlessly. Thereafter I have never had a good opinion about the much publicised magnanimity of the adults, especially, the farming community: they are quite mean hearted, essentially when it comes to even paltry sacrifices, false glorification of the peasant community's broad-heartedness, broad-mindedness, simplicity and magnanimity in the fine arts and literature, notwithstanding.

XXX

47. *Holee, Kolhoo And Dhooriyaa Maamaa*

Enter Protagonist

In the profusely fertile soil of my *Nanihaal,* the prominent crops that were grown normally were wheat, maize, millet, sugarcane, pulses of various kinds, vegetables and fruits. The area was not any less than an Elysium, both flora and fauna-wise!

For sugarcane was grown, and sugarcane has harvesting period of one year, its crop was harvested, or cut, from the month of October every year, and it was taken to the domestic crushers – the *Kolhoo* – for crushing and making the jaggery and powdered jaggery by boiling the sugarcane juice in huge cauldrons on very big hearths. For sugarcane was grown profusely in the area, in turn, owing to the area being replete with water – both underground and rain-water – the *Kolhoos* were installed in our *Nanihaal* too.

The cane crushing season, however, continued till, or far beyond, the festival of *Holee* and people would use the crusher by turns to make jaggery out of the cane juice produced in their fields. On one such *Holee*, when I was quite young, I was in my *Nanihaal.* The season was still pretty cold unlike nowadays when it's all summer throughout the year. The hamlet being quite small with population of only a few dozen people, the camaraderie amongst them was very intimate and intense. And festivals were celebrated with real fervour, too.

There was one evil spirit, too, in that hamlet, called *Dhooriyaa*. We addressed him by the appellation *'Dhooriyaa Maamaa'*. He was a petty thief; he used to steal goods from the passing goods trains running on the nearby railway track. Normally he stole the iron pipes that were used for boring handpumps in villages. *Dhooriyaa* was expert in climbing onto the carriages of running goods trains at night and after getting on top, he would throw the pipes in the fields beside the railway track. And when he could have thrown five or six pipes, he would dismount from the running train safely, and walking on foot only would collect all the pipes thus thrown, and later on would sell them in the nearby villages. He in fact had no qualms of conscience in this regard; rather, he prided in this sinful pursuit of his. The populace too surprisingly was supportive of and all praise for him – whether out of his dread or really out of reverence for his extraordinary valour I can't decide – possibly for they got their required pipes in their area itself which otherwise would have to be bought and brought from the town almost twenty five kms away. In a sense he was not treated as an abominable character, rather alike a Robin Hood, and commanded quite a respect in the area. His name in fact literally meant 'alike the dust', but by deeds he was nowhere near the dust.

But one thing is for sure that he was not well off despite all those thefts he indulged in almost regularly; he was ever in the state of hand to mouth. Possibly Nature had disposed his misdeeds like that. He had lost his wife long back, most likely under mental strain thinking that her husband was a thief, despite himself being a *Braahman.* His younger brother had died untimely, too, sometime thereafter. And the thinking adults of the area thought it expedient to arrange an unarranged, unconventional, marriage of the widower – *Dhooriyaa* – and the

widow of his younger brother, under what gospel truth or following which social norm I could never fathom. The complications of this unmatched and bizarre marriage were the stuff of gossip throughout the village in later years of their live-in arrangement. But that episode sometime later herein.

What I am intending to mention here is that on one such *Holee* occasion, *Dhooriyaa* was in his mettle having drunken a whit or having consumed the *Bhaang* – a local herb which was intoxicating -- and was chasing people for playing *Holee* with. He somehow was under obligation of my *Naanaajee* and had high regards for the members of our *Naanaa's* family. Who would not, of a well off and strongmen's family?

Our elder *Maamaajee's* son looked like a prince incarnate, both by personality and by countenance. He was darling of all and was very tender as well; also, because he was the eldest scion of the joint family. There is no doubt that the pedigree of theirs was quite influential and great. That was why people paid regards to them.

Dhooriyaa caught sight of *Maamaajee's* son and set off chasing him. *Maamaajee's* son ran fast and started moving along the bullocks pulling the log of the crusher around the pivot of the crusher – round and round. *Dhooriyaa* in a mock inebriated condition kept chasing him around the *Kolhoo* but could not catch hold of the sprightful lad. Other elders of the family were also present there at the *Kolhoo* engaged as they were in the crushing pursuit, but *Dhooriyaa* couldn't gather cudgels to throw mud on them – in villages only mud was the item with which the *Holee* was played, no colour business! I being present there was taking the mockery as real one, and something dreadful, too. When he sighted me standing there nonchalantly, *Dhooriyaa* pounced upon me, to my horror. I fled from there frightened, my *Naanee* adding to my fright by commenting mockingly, 'Do run away, lad, lest *Dhooriyaa* should drench you in dirty puddle!' Anyway, *Dhooriyaa maamaa* – he was also my *maamaa* in relation – did not catch me, even as, he never intended to; nor was he serious about catching the son of *Maamaajee*; he was simply celebrating the *Holee,* the festival of fun, by having fun with children.

Nevertheless, I was thinking that all those histrionics were real, but later on I realised that all that was merely a drama, an acting, as all other actions of our lives are: merely drama, *sans* any substance!

XXX

48. Barefoot's Fancy For Footwears

Enter Protagonist

As usual, we were at our *Naanee*'s. We seldom found anything memorable about our paternal side except wretchedness and grim circumstances and bloated arrogance, however, fake as well as sham. I was quite small and possibly ever bare-footed; I didn't use to have footwears, that is, *chappals.* Being barefoot for the babies and children, as also, for the poor elder ones was not a matter of wonder or an abnormality those days. We babes did not even know the implications of being barefooted. Even later in my life, I found my mother without any footwears throughout her youth and life, particularly, during her husband's reign: the latter could not afford even two morsels of food; how could he entertain such profligacies as footwears for her wife, or for issues, for that matter!

However, one day I noticed that other elders were seen wearing footwears while walking on the soil; even the son of my *Maamaajee* who was my age was having footwears. Only I was without *chappals.* I fancied for *chappals,* too. How to arrange them? I asked this question to my mother, "Where are my *chappals,* mother?"

"You don't have *chappals.*"

"Why? *Daadaa* has."

"We shall ask *Maamaajee* to fetch you *chappals* next time when he comes from the town."

My younger *Maamaajee* had a job at the town and visited the village every weekend. I became glad with this small answer from my mother. I couldn't notice at that age that my mother did not say that she would ask my father for fetching me *chappals*. She relied on her brother instead. This small episode has broad implications in social science and financial management. She didn't have slightest faith in the financial wherewithal of my paternal side: they all seemed to be self-centred and callous persons as regards household as well as family responsibilities. That was the bane of feudal thinking and feudal philosophy.

I relished the pleasant fancy of getting good soothing *chappals* the coming Saturday. And I narrated this dream to my playmates umpteen number of times, "Next time I shall have *chappals*, my *Maamaajee* will bring me new *chappals*."

It was a wintry morning and a bit foggy. I had woken up and gone to loo in the agricultural fields. After throwing up I was sitting at the banks of a waterway washing my buttocks when I sighted my younger *Maamaajee* coming from afar – also having finished his morning routine of throwing up or loo. I became very glad. In the foregoing evening I had not got chance to observe that *Maamaajee*

had come yesterday itself in the night: he plied by night train to and fro the town actually.

I was half finished washing, when *Maamaajee* came nearby. In my over excitement I asked, "*Maamaajee Raam-Raam! Maamaajee,* have you brought my *chappals*?" I was dead sure, he would have certainly brought my *chappals* as he had assured last time when he left for the town and my *Mameejee* had solicited him sincerely to fetch *chappals* for me, too. But to my surprise, *Maamaajee* neither acknowledged my salutations nor did he affirm that he had brought my *chappals*. I became sad: *Maamaajee* was not of that sort, he was of gentle mien normally.

I brought up the issue of non-compliance by *Maamaajee* with my mother at home in that as against her promise that my *chappals* would come next weekend, *Maamaajee* had not brought them. Mother had no plausible answer except that her brother had forgotten to bring the same. However, my *Maameejee* once again solicited the matter to *Maamaajee* pleading that he ought to have brought my baby *chappals* that I fancied so much. *Maamaajee* instead complained that I was saying *Raam-Raam* while at the same time washing my buttocks in the waterway, the brook. Then I realised why *Maamaajee* did not respond to my early morning obeisance to him:

that one should not pay regards to anybody while at the same time indulging in obscene activities like cleaning or wiping one's buttocks!

The *chappals* did not arrive for many weeks thereafter, too, and I lost all hope. However, later on those arrived; and before I could get enthralled, they got snapped, too. So fragile! Then I realised the futility of desiring anything if one did not have the wherewithal to afford the same. Almost throughout my childhood and youth I was without footwears in my village. Only when outdoors, away from the village, did I wear the footwears, that too, sparingly so that the rare commodity did not get destroyed before time.

XXX

49. Bhonpoo! (Loud-Speaker!)

Enter Protagonist

However harsh and unaffable might have been my real *Naanaa*'s demeanour, his elder cousin, our elder *Naanaajee,* was comparatively an affectionate personality – at least that was the impression gathered by me -- he oftentimes engaged with us children chatting in childlike manner. His countenance and stature was like that of a local lord: a warlord, a landlord. He had full command over his clan and himself.

In my babyhood, I and my younger sister – immediately next, younger to me -- had a very high sense of self-esteem and righteousness verging on fastidiousness, with the result that whenever somebody reprimanded us or punished us without a cause or even mistakenly, we reacted violently, rather, extremely vociferously: in a very high pitched voice, using full power of our lungs to shout at the offender, most of the time, my mother, *"Chaun maar rahee hai?"* (Why are you punishing us without any cause?). And it used to be a great embarrassment for my mother, ramifications of which being that in that tiny hamlet my voice resonated in all the nooks and corners of every household including in the ears of my decidedly tyrant maternal uncle. This melodrama gave the latter an added fuel for burning his heart and the mind of others, particularly, of my mother. My mother, I felt, was always at the receiving end so far as the misdemeanour of elder *Maamaa* was concerned.

One day when I was making abnormal noise of shouts, one of my playmates, *Vinod*, the grandson of our elder *Naanaajee,* was standing there; he told my mother that his grandfather was saying to him that "*Phool*'s children are *Bhonpoos* (loudspeakers)!" Hearing this chastising commentary, especially, from the side of my favourite adult, I got disillusioned, for heretofore I had the impression that everybody whosoever heard my bravado in the manner of shouting was all praise for me: this was not so, I realised. Nobody likes an anarchist and a misbehaved child or person!

XXX

50. Kanchhedan (*Ear-pricking*) (*Over To* Gurukul)

Enter Protagonist

One afternoon when we kids were busy playing, going on there in the homesteads was a frenzy of festive activity: the purifying or smearing of courtyard with cow-dung, the decorating of the same with dry coloured powders, the preparations of sweetmeats, the palpable presence or attendance of the serving classes around, like, barbers and scavengers and *band-waalaas*.

We were glad to observe all this merry-making going around our residential compound – the *Baakhar*. Something was going to take place, something great; we were also being dressed colourfully: me and my cousin – almost of the same age group.

Then on a wooden plank, my cousin was made to sit and the *panditjee* – the family priest -- chanted some ambiguous as well as unintelligible *mantras* accompanied with the folk songs sung by house-hold ladies. I felt envious that my cousin was being felicitated and was the focus of attention of everybody whilst I was not.

Suddenly, my cousin cried piercingly: the barber had pricked his ears with hot needle when his grand-mother was feigning to feed him sweetmeats. This was a *sanskaar* (rite) – *Kanchhedan sanskaar*. So painful! So dreadful it was! My envy towards my cousin was gone instantly!

Before I could draw solace that at least it was not me who was being subjected to this man-made cruelty as well as violence, I found myself at the centre of focus. My heart started pounding at the prospect of facing the same sort of carnival being played with me, upon my tender ears. Soon and swiftly my ears were pierced, too. Of course, on the pretext of feeding sweetmeats simultaneously.

Once the rite was solemnised, we heaved a sigh of relief -- me and my cousin. We were now supposedly grown-ups, certified ones; we had now worn *up-weet – janeyoo* (the thread of wisdom and abstinence)! The family elders explained to us for our solace that we were now *dwij-* the reborn, that we were now the part of our clan, and also, that we could now go to the *Gurukul* (the abode of learning, the literacy).

XXX

The End

English Books by *'Videh'*

Hypocrisy & Reality (fiction series: 9 books)

'Hypocrisy & Reality' is a fiction series comprising multiple books – novels. The fiction is aimed at depicting the hypocrisy of human society in every respect, be it the upbringing and treatment of babies, toddlers, children, adolescents, youths, or be it the treatment meted out to adults, aged ones, those who are closely related with oneself, with one's blood; not to speak of those called strangers or outsiders. Barring a rarity, nobody cares two hoots for the sentiments or security and safety of other living creatures on this sole planet nurturing 'living' beings!

Book 1: Beyond the Pale (fiction)

'Beyond the Pale' of Time & Space is the first volume of the long fiction series 'Hypocrisy & Reality' and as the name suggests, it deals with the timespan in the life of the protagonist when one had not even had a tryst with the concepts of Time and Space, nor did they make any difference in one's life if those ubiquitous phenomena were not taken cognizance of. Those were the years before the realm of schooling, the arena of perfect unconcern for the written letters, words, or numbers.

Book 2: Wilderness of Literacy (fiction)

'Wilderness of Literacy' is the second volume in the long fiction series 'Hypocrisy & Reality' and, as the name suggests, it takes the protagonist in the arena of letters, words, and numbers: the realm of what we call the 'literacy'. The experience of a child while treading this seemingly dreaded as well as untrodden landscape is nothing short of venturing into a wilderness; of course, led and mentored first by one's parents and thereafter invariably by their preceptors -- the masters -- all of whom have a tremendous amount of impact on the future human being that emerges from their inputs given and endeavours made towards making a man, the humanity.

Book 3: Advent of Time (fiction)

'Advent of Time' is the third volume in the long fiction series entitled 'Hypocrisy & Reality' and covers the schooling period when the protagonist discovered the phenomenon of Time, and also, figuratively he felt that it was then his time, even as, he mysteriously discovered his latent potential and wisdom catapulting himself into the uppermost orbits of glory, fame and all round applause from his classmates, masters as well as teachers. To his own amazement as well as bewilderment! Nevertheless, this providential blessing was not without its blemishes in the shape of rancour and envy of fellow classmates and their patrons towards him. Even as, Nature never allows anybody pleasure and praise without at the same time associating with them the equivalent amount of pain and back-biting!

Book 4: Devoid of Shelter (fiction)

'Devoid of Shelter', the fourth volume in the long fiction series 'Hypocrisy & Reality' furthers the journey of the protagonist into the world where he discovered to his dismay that he had no place on the globe which he could call as his home; he had no place of his own where he could take shelter during the day, and during the night. He somehow made do with seeking shelter with the relatives – maternal chiefly; not as a transitory phenomenon, but for good, until he himself took command of his life, snatching himself away from the indolent lifestyle of his parents. He also discovered during the refuge that however meritorious one might be, without the good base of ancestry, one was not considered as such.

Book 5: Price of Refuge (fiction)

'Price of Refuge', the fifth volume in the fiction series 'Hypocrisy & Reality' furthers the journey of the protagonist into the world when he returned to his paternal relatives and found to his dismay that his father was absolutely incapable of arranging a dwelling of his own. Also, he found himself to be a mute subject to child abuse at the hands of none other than supposedly an elder cousin of his, the son of his so-called benefactors who provided refuge in their vacant house. That was the price paid by the child for the indolence and handicaps of an unworthy father for seeking shelter under the tutelage of so-called relatives. No refuge seemingly looking innocuous goes without some price to be paid either by self, spouse or one's children.

Book 6: Hatred towards Love (fiction)

'Hatred towards Love', the sixth volume in the fiction series 'Hypocrisy & Reality' furthers the journey of the protagonist into the world where to his amusement he found himself catapulted into the realm of a celebrity or at least a child prodigy as far as the small rural catchment area was concerned. By virtue of his giftedness in the realm of studies and his bewitching countenance, the classmates, especially, the lasses of her age could not help restraining themselves from loving him; and they did it overtly, without caring for the opinions and feelings of other class-fellows. Albeit the protagonist himself wallowed in the faulty ideology that having any truck with fair sex was anathema and a great sin which could not be washed away in later life.

Book 7: Towards the Yoga (fiction)

'Towards the Yoga', the seventh volume in the fiction series 'Hypocrisy & Reality' dwells on the period in the journey of life of the protagonist when he was at the pinnacle of his bodily prowess and psychic acuity, thanks to his habit of pursuing *Yogaasans* regularly as well as religiously. As though something divine was associated with the pursuit of *Yogaasans*, his father luckily could get an *ad hoc* teacher's job in the town school too; however, that was not to be sustained throughout for at the fag-end of the academic session, his father fell out with the Principal of school and was expelled. *Yoga,* nevertheless, gave the protagonist a hue that was unparallelled, and which materialised into the worldly as well as societal fame for him.

Book 8: On the Descent (fiction)

'On the Descent', the eighth volume in the fiction series 'Hypocrisy & Reality' takes the protagonist over the hump. He was then a ward of such a guardian who did not have any wherewithal to run his household, yet had no qualms about begetting more issues, more and more at that. Agriculture, of course, he had as an inheritance but he was by nature averse to anything even distantly associated with agriculture or Nature, for that matter. Any industrious as well as expedient agriculturalist would have eked out one's livelihood quite easily from the fifteen *beeghaa*s of arable land his father had inherited from his resourceful, brave as well as powerful ancestors, but not he.

Book 9: In the Exile (fiction)

'In the Exile', the ninth volume in the fiction series 'Hypocrisy & Reality' furthers the journey of the protagonist into the world where post his dramatic jump into the orbit of fame in the wake of his High School result, he found himself entirely in a barren land where he could see no ray of hope from his father, even as, the latter was totally incapable of arranging the means to further the studies for his exceptionally gifted son. For the first time, the protagonist realised that his father was incapable of meeting his requirements for pursuing further studies. He was already suffering emotionally having been separated from his mother for the first time! This was for him like an exile, that too, very uncomfortable!

Bewailing Muse (poetry)

Be it the sage *Valmeeki* or be it the modern poet *Sumitraa Nandan Pant*, both have held that poetry has its founts in heart and is the outcome of extreme sorrow, misery or pangs of separation. Poetry cannot be created; it gets engendered out of compulsion. From the heart! Heart's language is poetry or musing! I have offered to christen them as Muse: 'Bewailing Muse'; the first musings out of wailings! Nevertheless, I am tempted not to treat them as

children's literature for I sense some substantial element, too, in them. The period of the composition of these poems is from 1972 to 1976; and I feel that my wailings have not fallen on deaf ears, so to say, given my present circumstances of life which are totally opposite to the then prevailing ones!

Chambellion (drama: comedietta)

In the genre of Drama (Comedietta), here is the playlet *'Chambellion'* that exposes the bizarre reality of the political developments post transfer of reins from the whites to the yellow people in the guise of 'Democracy' and 'Independence'; whereas actually the latter have been pursuing their dynastic agenda and propagating their own family fiefdoms that have flourished like weeds in multitudes in the void created by annihilation of Princely states and Landlords. Allegorically, it may be compared with the weed flourishing in an agricultural field which has remained unsown after harvest of the previous crop. For the subjects, verily, there is no Freedom whatsoever, in literal sense.

Brainy Beasts (short stories)

This is an anthology of short stories, included wherein are four short stories or farces, so to say, that is, anecdotes including the 'In An Illegible Script', which is the English version of the author's *Hindee* short story *'Anpadh Lipi Mein...* (अनपढ़ लिपि में)' that was first published in now extinct though the then prestigious *Hindee* magazine the 'Kaadambinee' way back in July, 1992, with quite an applause and accolades from the sides of kind readers! Other stories or anecdotes are also those published in other places, i.e. journals of variegated hues. Nothing uttered in these works is meaningless; this conviction is at work behind the inspiration to publish them in book form for kind readers.

Search for Life (translation of 'Hatyaaree Sadee Mein Jeevan Kee Khoj' (हत्यारी सदी में जीवन की खोज))

English Translation by *'Videh' Arvind Kumar* of *Hindee* poetry book *'Hatyaaree Sadee Mein Jeevan Kee Khoj'* (हत्यारी सदी में जीवन की खोज) by renowned young poet *'Nirvikaar' Mukesh Kumar*. This book has earned *'Nirvikaar'* the award of *'Jai Shankar Prasaad Puraskaar'* of Rs. One Lac from the *'Rajya Karmchaaree Saahitya Sansthaan, Uttar Pradesh'*. On the *Hindee* book *'Hatyaaree Sadee Mein Jeevan Kee Khoj,'* critiques by renowned personalities -- both young and old -- like *Ashwaghosh, Prempaal Sharmaa, Rajeev Saxena, Dr Anoop Singh, Dr Devkee Nandan Sharmaa, Manoj Kumaar Jhaa, Gautam Rajarshi,* etc have been published in various journals and magazines. The renowned critic Dr *Om Nishchal* has included this anthology in the select category for *'Kavya Paridrishya'* of 2017 amongst the famous poetry books.

Reality of Invisible (translation of 'Adrishya Kaa Yathaarth' (अदृश्य का यथार्थ))

English translation by *'Videh' Arvind Kumar* of the *Hindee* poetry book *'Adrishya Kaa Yathaarth'* (अदृश्य का यथार्थ) by renowned poet *'Ashwaghosh'*

Om Prakaash Sharmaa. 'Ashwaghosh' -- a well-known moniker of *Hindee* world! A litterateur of impeccable renown! Praised by multitudes -- both in literary and plebeian spheres! He has been composing prolifically -- having published over two dozen books spanning all the genre! The thesis, the short stories, the short epics, the anthologies, the new genre songs, the *ghazals*, the poetry for children *et al.* Covering all age groups! He has been honoured with many awards in literary and academic fields by prestigious institutions.

Nagasaki: Bomb & Aftermath (commentary on the first novel of Nobel Laureate, Kazuo Ishiguro) (Displayed on Oxford bookstore)

This is a work of literary study into the first novel 'The Pale View of Hills' by 2017 Literature Nobel Laureate, Kazuo Ishiguro, who has narrated in a mesmerising style of story telling the tale of Japanese society undergoing change in the aftermath of dropping of atomic bomb. The Americans not only vanquished and occupied the Japanese military and land by dropping the most lethal weapon never before heard of – the atomic bomb – on two of the Japanese cities, one of which was Nagasaki which witnessed this technological devastation on 8th of August, 1945, but also, occupied the minds and hearts of Japanese youth, both men and women. The youth of Japan started decrying everything old and conventional including their erstwhile education system and the ideologies of patriotism and nationalism.

Procreation, the Adorable (English summary of Shiv Puraan)

The *Shiva-ling* has ever been a matter of amazement and mystery for mankind. That something obscure is there behind the adoration of such a carnal symbol as *ling* irrespective of the same being that of a deity called *Shiva* has ever been lingering in my mind. Why should a large majority of population in this land – from north to south -- worship the genitals so openly, so brazenly? So reverently! *Shiva* is supposed to be a mythological persona, in existence too long back in time, who might have been the pioneer in realizing the spectacular qualities of *ling* and *yoni,* specifically, those of converting the *sthaavar* (the insensate) into *jangam* (the sensate) and those of creating the *satva-lok,* (conscious beings).

Self-Styled Sovereign, the Judiciary (Dramatic deliberation on the state of judiciary)

This is in fact an academic deliberation on the functioning and reality of the judicial system prevalent in India post what they euphemistically call the 'Independence' or, literally, the *'Aazaadee'.* Whose Independence was it anyway? For whom? Except for the ruling class? The lawyers first, and then the hooligans of *Chambal.* Nonetheless, the judiciary of the free country turned out to be one step further than its new crop of leaders; they usurped the entire authority from the latter in subtle moves one after the other. In olden epochs, the autocratic *Sultaans* or *Baadshaahs* dispensed justice purely depending upon their whims and fancies, which were incidental to the moods and tantrums of the Sovereign. Historically as well, the Real Sovereign was the one who dispensed justice. The Judiciary in Indian Republic soon realised this and acted.

XXX

'विदेह' रचित हिंदी ग्रंथ

अनपढ़ लिपि (कहानी-संग्रह)

'विदेह' अरविन्द कुमार की आठ हिंदी कहानियों का संकलन! संकलन की पहली कहानी 'अनपढ लिपि में ...' जुलाई, 1992 में प्रतिष्ठित हिंदी पत्रिका 'कादंबिनी' में छपी थी। सिग्नेचर' भी स्वच्छता के प्रति सरकारी महकमे की विद्रूपात्मक मनोदशा का कड़वा चित्रण है। 'ताकि आप अपने पक्ष में रहें!' नये प्रकार के कर्मचारियों की मानसिकता को इंगित करती है। फिर फिर वही लोग' भेड़-बकरियों की तरह दुरुपयोग किये जा रहे जन-समुदाय के विषय में कहानी है। 'अपार्थाइड' : वस्तुतः तो, शक्तिशाली और निर्बल का भेद ही असली रंग-भेद है। 'नया वेद' 'आज़ादी' नाम से वही पारम्परिक पद्धति चतुराई-पूर्वक 'नया संविधान' के नाम से चलाये जाने की पोल-पट्टी खोलती है। 'पहली कमाई' कहानी का आख्यान कल्पना से भी अधिक विस्मयकारी है! 'भगवान को पैसा' समाज और सरकार दोनों ही की धन के प्रति जो दृष्टि है, उस पर तीखा व्यंग्य है।

पाषाण-युग (कहानी-संग्रह)

'विदेह' अरविन्द कुमार की सात हिंदी कहानियों का संकलन! संकलन की पहली कहानी 'ब्लॉक का पेड़' आज के समाज में क्षीण होते हुए आपसी सौहार्द्र, एवं अजनबियों के प्रति बढ़ते अकारण वैमनस्य, को बिंबित करती हुई सच्चाई है। मेरी

ज्ञाति' भारत में जातियों के हास्यास्पद 'प्रहसन' – फ़ार्स (farce) -- को चित्रित करके इसकी विद्रूपता को व्यंजित करती है। 'हिंदू-मुसलमान' साम्प्रदायिकता के प्रश्न को व्यक्तियों – दो घनिष्ठ मित्रों -- के स्तर पर परीक्षण करके देखती है। 'मुर्गबाज' समय की नब्ज पर हाथ रखने की कोशिश है। 'मंदिरों, मस्जिदों, गुरुद्वारों, गिरजाघरों में ...' साम्प्रदायिक कट्टरता की निरर्थकता को व्यंजित करने के लिए है, जो मृत्यु के पर्दे के पीछे कितनी हास्यास्पद बन जाती है! ऐ अधर्मी!' आदमी की नश्ल को बदलने की नाहक कोशिश कही जा सकती है। 'राक्षस' इस नये शासन-प्रशासन में व्याप्त भ्रष्टाचार पर एक व्यंग्यात्मक टिप्पणी है, और बताती है कि राक्षस कोई कपोल-कल्पना नहीं है, बल्कि आज भी एक वास्तविकता है।

निसर्ग (कहानी-संग्रह)

'विदेह' अरविन्द कुमार की सात हिंदी कहानियों का संकलन! संकलन की पहली कहानी 'मुलाक़ात एक बड़े लेखक से' एक बड़े लेखक और एक आम आदमी के जीवन के साम्य और अंतर दोनों को ही उजागर करती है। 'फाड़ी हुई कविता' एक ऐसे पति की व्यथा-कथा है, जो एक कवि एवं साहित्यकार भी है। 'नया साल' में कुछ भी नया नहीं होता, फिर भी सारी दुनिया किस कदर बाबली हुई रहती है। 'हितैषिणी' शादी जैसी संस्थाओं के पाखण्ड, फ़रेब एवं परम्पराओं से चिपकाव की विद्रूपता पर सशक्त प्रहार करती है। 'छोटे-से शरीर में कैदी' शिशुमन की विवशता को चित्रित करती है; वह पूरी तरह माँ-बाप की मूर्खताओं पर निर्भर रहने को विवश है। 'निसर्ग' एक रोमांटिक कहानी है। 'टूट-टूटकर गिरते सितारे' दिखाती है कि कैसे समाज अपने ही शिकंजे में फँसा रहकर ही परेशान होता रहता है!

आर्त-गान (कविता-संग्रह)

'वियोगी होगा पहला कवि, आह से उपजा होगा गान
उमड़कर आँखों से चुपचाप, बही होगी कविता अनजान!'
(सुमित्रा नंदन पंत)
या

'मा निषाद त्वम् गम: प्रतिष्ठाम् शाश्वती समा:
यत् क्रौंच मिथुनादेकम् त्वम् वधी: काम मोहितम्!'
(महर्षि वाल्मीकि)

चाहे तो आदि कवि वाल्मीकि हों, चाहे फिर छायावादी कवि पंत हों, एक बात तो तय है, कि कविता वियोग या विषाद या शोक से उत्सृजित होती है। पहले-पहल की रचनाएँ हैं ये – जीवन के पहले-प्रहर की; अतः बच्चों के उपयुक्त ही हो सकती हैं। बाल-कविता! बाल-कविता इसे मैंने फिर भी इसलिए नहीं कहा है, क्योंकि इनमें मुझे कुछ सार भी सन्निहित लगता रहा है; एकदम तो बकवास नहीं ही हैं ये, जैसी कि बाल (अबोध) - कविता की प्रकृति और प्रवृत्ति होती है। ये कविताएँ 1972 से 1976 के काल-खंड में सृजित हैं; और अभी लगभग अर्ध-शती की परिपक्व दृष्टि से भी परिमार्जित!

काल-क्रंदन (कविता-संग्रह)

जीवन के प्रथम प्रहर की हृदयाभिव्यक्तियों (1972 से 1976 तक) के 'आर्त-गान' के बाद, 1979 से 1990 तक के द्वादश वर्षीय काल-खण्ड में मैंने जो क्रंदन किया था, उसे मैंने कविता कहा; और उन कविताओं का 'काल-रेख' नाम मैंने चुना था; क्योंकि काल की छाती पर 12 वर्षों तक मैं जो घिसटता रहा था, उस लकीर पीटने को 'काल-रेख' कहना ही मुझे रुच रहा था। परन्तु, कुछ काव्यात्मक स्फुरणा के वश, कुछ काल-अंतराल के प्रभाव-वश मैं अब इसे 'काल-क्रंदन' ही कहना अधिक समीचीन समझ रहा हूँ। साहित्य -- और इसीलिए कविता भी -- जीवन के मूल की अर्थात् सत्य की खोज है: सत्य की परख, यथार्थ की परख! इसमें सब कुछ सुनने-सुनाने, गाने-गवाने ही योग्य है, ऐसा दावा मैं नहीं करता। परन्तु, क्या पढ़ने-पढ़ाने योग्य है, और क्या नहीं, इसका निर्णय भी तो मैं नहीं कर सकता; क्योंकि इसका कण-कण मेरा नितांत निजी सच है! इसमें कितना किस और किसी का भी सच प्रस्तुत है, यह निर्णय उन्हीं पर!

अननुभूत काल (कविता-संग्रह)

अब यह तीसरी काव्य-पुस्तक है! एकदम नवीन काल से सम्बंधित! अभी-अभी हो गुज़रे बड़े मानवीय हादसे को रेखांकित करती हुई: कोरोना की महा-आपदा! विश्व-आपदा! जो न कभी हुई

थी, और आशा एवम् प्रार्थना ही कर सकते हैं, न कभी भविष्य में होगी! एकदम नये रूप में दुनिया को सोचने को मजबूर होना पड़ा: 'ऐसा भी हो सकता है?' बेतहाशा भागम-भाग में लगी दुनिया अचानक रुक-सी गयी; नहीं, रुक ही गयी – शब्दशः। वायुयान रुक गये, रेलयान रुक गये, बसें रुक गयीं, सारे वाहन रुक गये। मंदिर, मश्जिद, गुरुद्वारे और चर्च भी बंद हो गये: परमात्मा के घर थे वे! हैं! मक्का, मदीना बंद हो गये। वेटिकन बंद हो गया। वह चिरंतन अटूट आस्था जो रुकने का नाम नहीं लेती थी, और आए-दिन छोटी-छोटी बातों पर सिर-फुटव्वल को बेताब रहती थी, अचानक अपने को सकपकाता हुआ पाने लगी। क्या वह बस आस्था ही भर थी, दुनियावी प्राणियों को भरमाने के लिए; क्या उसमें कोई पारमार्थिक सार न था? तार्किक मन यह सोचने को विवश हो गया। इस कोरोना-काल ने बहुत सारे पाखण्ड-मण्डन किये हैं!

अम्बेडकर-स्मृति (नाटिका)

जाति की समस्या भारत देश के लिए भयंकर होती जा रही है। यह जाति ही है जिसके चलते भारत-भूमि आक्रांताओं के समक्ष प्रणत हो गयी थी। कड़वी सच्चाई यह है कि राजनीतिक चतुराई के चलते 'सत्ताधीशों' ने अपने आप को 'ऊँचा' और सत्ता से 'वंचित' जनों को 'नीचा' मानना शुरू कर दिया। 'आज़ादी' के अधकचरे प्रयोग के चलते स्थिति और भी भयावह हो गयी है; 'नीचे लोग' ऊँचे लोगों को गरियाते रहते हैं: उसके लिए वे 'मनु-स्मृति' नाम की किसी पौराणिक पुस्तक को गरियाते रहते हैं, जबकि वास्तविकता यह है कि आधुनिक भारत के 99.99 प्रतिशत लोगों ने उस पुस्तक का पढ़ना तो दूर, नाम तक नहीं सुना है। उधर, नये सत्ताधीशों ने नयी स्मृति लिखकर -- संविधान लिखकर (जिसकी ड्राफ्टिंग समिति के अध्यक्ष होने के नाते अम्बेडकर को श्रेय मिला हुआ है) – पूर्ववर्ती समाज-व्यवस्था एवं अर्थ-व्यवस्था को एक सिरे से नकार और नेस्तनाबूद कर दिया है। समाज के बीच इस पर जो बहस चल रही है, उसी का एक छोटा सा नमूना है यह एकांकी!

प्रिय-प्रवास (संकलन, 'हरिऔध' के महाकाव्य का)

'प्रिय-प्रवास' हिंदी -- खड़ी बोली -- का प्रथम महाकाव्य है, जो स्वनाम धन्य महाकवि अयोध्या सिंह उपाध्याय 'हरिऔध' की अमर कृति है। अत्यंत सुमधुर काव्य के रूप में युग-पुरुष श्रीकृष्ण के गोकुल से मथुरा प्रवास और उनके वियोग से व्यथित गोकुल-वासियों की विरह-वेदना का सरस चित्रण इसमें है। वह एक प्रकार से हर प्राणी की वेदना ही है, जो वह उस समय अनुभव करता है जब कोई स्वजन प्रवास हेतु जाता है या प्रयाण करता है, जो कि संसृति का अपरिहार्य लक्षण ही है। आसक्ति, मोह और ममता सब दुःखों का मूल है; जबकि ज्ञान दुःखों से मुक्ति का साधन! इस महा-आख्यान का यही सार अथच् केंद्रीय संदेश समझ में आता है! 'प्रिय-प्रवास' विरह, बिछुड़ने की वेदना, नैसर्गिक प्रेम और विश्व-कल्याण के संदेश का ही महाकाव्यात्मक सरस रूप है। 'विदेह' अरविन्द कुमार ने इस अद्भुत साहित्यिक कृति को पुनर्संकलित एवं पुनर्मुद्रित करके इसकी एक संक्षिप्त गद्य-कथा भी इसमें प्रस्तुत की है।

प्रार्थना एवं प्राणांश (संकलित प्रेरक काव्यांश)

बहुत ही सरस और सार्थक प्रार्थनाओं एवं प्रेरणादायी काव्यांशों का संचयन है यह! जो न जाने कहाँ-कहाँ से 'विदेह' अरविंद कुमार ने अपनी रुचि अनुकूल संकलित एवं सम्पादित किया है, उन सभी मनीषियों के प्रति हार्दिक आभार व्यक्त करते हुए, जिनकी रचनाएँ और रचनाओं के प्राणांश इसमें संकलित किये गये हैं। जीवन, मृत्यु के वाहन के आगमन की प्रतीक्षा में रत यात्री के कार्य-कलाप और मनोदशा के अतिरिक्त और क्या है! इस प्रतीक्षा में क्या-क्या अनहोनी अनुभूतियाँ नहीं होतीं! इस प्रतीक्षा को कम कष्टकर करने के लिए काव्य-शास्त्र अनुश्रवण की अनुशंसा मनीषियों ने की है। साथ ही, प्रार्थना के माहात्म्य को भी स्वीकारा है।

मनो पुब्बंगमा धम्मा, मनो सेट्ठा मनोमया!'
भगवान बुद्ध ने मन से ही सृजित होता हुआ इस सकल प्रपञ्च को बताया है। अत: मन को शुचि एवं निष्कंप रखकर आप संसार का अनुभव बदल सकते हैं। जब सभी कुछ कल्पित है, तो सबको अपना मत अनुभव जैसा ही लगता है। परन्तु, है वस्तुतः सब कुछ कपोल-कल्पित ही: न इसे सत्य कहने का कोई तात्पर्य है, न असत्य कहने का! बस मन को साधने का साधनभर है प्रार्थना!

महामुनि वाल्मीकि रचित् इतिहास : *उत्तरकाण्ड* (वाल्मीकि के उत्तरकाण्ड का गद्यांतरित सारांश)

'रामायण' आदिकाव्य है, न केवल भारतवर्ष का, अपितु सकल मानव-समाज का भी। महर्षि वाल्मीकि-कृत यह काव्य-पुस्तक वस्तुतः तत्कालीन इतिहास है: उस राजवंश का, जिसकी कीर्ति हज़ारों वर्ष पश्चात् भी आज तक अक्षुण्ण है। उस राजवंश के तत्कालीन यशस्वी सम्राट 'राम' का इसमें वर्णन है। राम-राज्य की व्यवस्था, जिसका वर्णन ऋषि ने किया है, आज भी शासन-व्यवस्था के हेतु आदर्श मानी जाती है।

लेखक ने संस्कृत के ग्रंथ का मात्र सार रूप यहाँ प्रस्तुत किया है; सब प्रकार की काव्यात्मकता और अतिशयोक्तियों का निवारण करते हुए। साथ ही, आलंकारिकता को आधुनिक संदर्भों से जोड़ते हुए ऐतिहासिक-वैज्ञानिक अर्थों में भी विषय को समझाने का प्रयास किया है।

कितना यह किसको भाता है, यह तो हर व्यक्ति की अपनी-अपनी रुचि और सोच पर निर्भर करेगा; बहरहाल, लेखक ने अपना दृष्टिकोण प्रस्तुत किया है, वह भी इस चिन्ता से कि नयी पीढ़ी अपनी बहुमूल्य विरासत – गौरवशाली इतिहास -- की ओर एकदम ध्यान नहीं दे रही है। उसका एक कारण ग्रंथों का संस्कृत में होना, और दूसरा अत्यधिक प्रतीकात्मक होने के कारण कपोल-कल्पित-सा लगना, भी हो सकता है; उसी कारण का निवारण करने का यह विनीत प्रयास है।

XXX

लेखक-परिचय

'विदेह' अरविन्द कुमार

भारतीय साहित्य की उदात्त पीठिका को आधुनिक संदर्भों से संपृक्त करने वाले सारस्वत साधक एवं विशिष्ट लेखन-शैली के प्रणेता वरिष्ठ साहित्यकार श्री अरविन्द कुमार 'विदेह' का जन्म 6 अप्रैल 1957 ई को उत्तर प्रदेश के गौतमबुद्धनगर जनपद की जेवर तहसील के छोटे-से गाँव 'मारहरा' में हुआ था। आपके माता-पिता की मानव-मूल्यों में गहरी आस्था रही है। सीमित संसाधनों, बल्कि विपन्नता, के बावजूद भी आप सफलता के लाभी हुए। आपने तत्कालीन आगरा विश्वविद्यालय के अलीगढ़ स्थित धर्मसमाज कॉलेज से भौतिक विज्ञान में स्नातकोत्तर उपाधि प्राप्त की है। आप देश के प्रतिष्ठित बैंक – भारतीय स्टेट बैंक – में दीर्घकालीन सेवा प्रदान करने के उपरांत दिसम्बर, 2018 में सहायक महाप्रबंधक के पद से सेवा निवृत्त हुए हैं।

श्री 'विदेह' छात्र-जीवन से ही अत्यंत मेधावी रहे हैं। विज्ञान-संवर्ग के विद्यार्थी होते हुए भी आपकी साहित्य के प्रति गहरी अभिरुचि रही है। साहित्य के प्रति आपका अनुराग इतना प्रबल रहा है कि बैंकिंग सेक्टर में अति व्यस्त जीवन-शैली वाली नौकरी करते हुए भी आप साहित्य और लेखन से अनवरत रूप से जुड़े रहे हैं। उनकी रचनाएँ तत्कालीन 'कादम्बिनी' जैसी लब्ध-प्रतिष्ठ पत्रिकाओं में काफ़ी पहले छप चुकी हैं; और उनके अन्य लेख एवं कविताएँ अन्य हिंदी, अंग्रेज़ी पत्र-पत्रिकाओं में यदा-कदा छपते रहे हैं। साथ ही, आपने हिंदी एवं अंग्रेजी भाषा के साहित्य का विशद अध्ययन एवं सृजन किया है। संस्कृत एवं पाली भाषा के साहित्य में भी आपकी गहरी अभिरुचि है।

विभिन्न विधाओं में आपने अब तक 27 ग्रंथों का प्रणयन किया है, जिनमें 17 अंग्रेजी एवं 10 हिंदी भाषा में हैं। हिंदी की पुस्तकों में 03 कहानी-संग्रह (अनपढ़ लिपि, पाषाण युग, निसर्ग); 03 कविता-संग्रह (आर्त-गान, काल-क्रन्दन, अननुभूत काल); 01 नाटिका (अम्बेडकर-स्मृति); 01 काव्य-संचयन (प्रार्थना एवं प्राणांश) उल्लेखनीय हैं। इसके अतिरिक्त आपने खड़ी बोली के प्रथम महाकाव्य 'प्रिय-प्रवास' को भी पुनर्संकलित एवं पुनर्मुद्रित किया है; तथा साथ ही, वाल्मीकि रामायण के उत्तरकाण्ड का गद्यांतरण इतिहास के दृष्टिकोण से आपने 'महामुनि

111

वाल्मीकि रचित् इतिहास: रामायण – उत्तरकाण्ड' नामक पुस्तक के रूप में किया है।

अंग्रेजी भाषा में आपकी उपन्यास श्रृंखला 'Hypocrisy & Reality' है जिसके अब तक 9 खण्ड वह प्रस्तुत कर चुके हैं (Beyond the Pale; Wilderness of Literacy; Advent of Time; Devoid of Shelter; Price of Refuge; Hatred towards Love; Towards the *Yoga*; On the Descent; In the Exile)। इसके अतिरिक्त, 01 Comedietta (*Chambellion*); 01 Short Story collection (Brainy Beasts); 01 Poetry anthology (Bewailing Muse); 01 Drama (Self-styled Sovereign, the Judiciary); पौराणिक ग्रंथ 'शिव-पुराण' के आधुनिक संदर्भों में अध्ययन पर आधारित 01 पुस्तक (Procreation, the Adorable); 2017 के साहित्य नोबेल पुरस्कार विजेता, Kazuo Ishiguro, के प्रथम उपन्यास 'A Pale View of the Hills' पर आधारित 01 समीक्षात्मक ग्रंथ (Nagasaki: Bomb & Aftermath) हैं।

'विदेह' जितने मौलिक सर्जक हैं उतने ही समर्थ अनुवादक भी हैं। उन्होंने हिंदी के 02 काव्य-संग्रहों – 'निर्विकार' मुकेश के 'हत्यारी सदी में जीवन की खोज', और 'अश्वघोष' ओमप्रकाश शर्मा के 'अदृश्य का यथार्थ' – का काव्यात्मक अनुवाद अंग्रेजी में किया है, जो क्रमश: 'Search for Life' एवं 'Reality of Invisible' के नाम से प्रकाशित हुई हैं।

'विदेह' के व्यक्तित्व का निर्माण घोर विपन्नता और कठोर संघर्षों ने किया है, जिसका प्रभाव उनकी लेखन-शैली पर निर्भीक अभिव्यक्ति और बेवाकी के रूप में देखा जा सकता है। आपके जीवन का अनुभव अत्यन्त व्यापक रहा है। आपने विपन्नता भी भोगी है, और सुख-सुविधा-सम्पन्न अमेरिकी जीवन भी जीया है; साथ ही, अनेक विदेश-यात्राओं का भी आपको अनुभव है।

केवल साहित्य ही नहीं, 'विदेह' की प्रवृत्तियों में ध्यान-साधना, विपश्यना, योग-साधना, प्राकृतिक-जीवन, आरोग्य, शाकाहार, बागवानी, पर्यटन और पैदल भ्रमण भी सम्मिलित हैं।

2024 के हिंदी दिवस पर – 14 सितंबर को – 'विदेह' को 'शुभम् साहित्य, कला एवम् संस्कृति संस्थान' द्वारा उनके सर्वोच्च सम्मान 'शुभम् रत्न' से सम्मानित किया गया।

'विदेह' की पुस्तकें 'Notion Press', Blue Rose One, Amazon और Flipkart पर तीनों ही प्रारूपों – ebooks, paperback एवम् hard cover – में उपलब्ध हैं।

XXX

About the Author

'Videh' Arvind Kumar

An unflinching adorer of the goddess of wisdom, the *Saraswatee*, and the one who has associated the lofty traditions of Indian literature with the present day contexts, and also, an author of an uncanny style of his own, the seasoned litterateur, *'Videh' Arvind Kumar,* was born on 6th of April, 1957, at a hamlet called *'Maar-Haraa'* in *Jewar Tehseel* of *Gautam Buddha Nagar* distt. in UP. His parents were staunch votaries of human values. Despite unbearable financial constraints, rather extreme wretchedness, he overcame the hurdles of existence and succeeded. He is a post-graduate in Physics from D S College, *Aleegarh*, affiliated to the then *Aagaraa* University. He retired as an Asstt General Manager from the esteemed Bank – State Bank of India – after putting in a long as well as illustrious service there.

'*Videh*' has been meritorious ever since his school days. Despite being a science stream scholar, he has been showing a keen interest in literature all along. His bonding with literature has been so strong that notwithstanding his pursuing such a busy job as Banking, he managed to sustain his love for literature. His works have been published decades back in the then esteemed magazines such as '*Kaadambinee*'. Also, his stray articles and compositions have found place in various magazines and journals now and then. Besides, he has been a voracious reader of literature and other stuff both in *Hindee* and English languages, apart from himself being a prolific writer and a poet. He is also an adorer of the literature in *Sanskrit* and *Pali* languages.

In variegated genre he has composed as many as 27 books so far, of which, 17 are in English and 10 in *Hindee*. Among the *Hindee* books, there are 03 story anthologies (*Anapadh Lipi; Paashaan Yug; Nisarg*); 03 poetry anthologies (*Aaart Gaan; Kaal Krandan; Ananubhoot Kaal*); 01 drama (*Ambedkar Smriti*); 01 collection of select poetic pieces (*Praarthanaa evam Praanaansh*). Aside of this, he has compiled, commented, edited and got re-published the first epic of the *Khadee Bolee Hindee*, the *Priya Pravaas*; and a book entitled '*Mahaamuni Vaalmeeki Rachit Itihaas: Raamaayan -- Uttar Kaand*' which presents, in succinct prose form, the ancient history of India as narrated in the most ancient epic.

As regards English oeuvre of '*Videh*', he has so far published 9 volumes of the long fiction series 'Hypocrisy & Reality' (Beyond the Pale; Wilderness of Literacy; Advent of Time; Devoid of Shelter; Price of Refuge; Hatred towards Love; Towards the *Yoga*; On the Descent; In the Exile) with yet more planned to come. Besides, 01 Comedietta (*Chambellion*); 01 Short Story collection (Brainy Beasts); 01 Poetry anthology (Bewailing Muse); 01 Drama (Self-Styled Sovereign, the Judiciary); 01 book based on the study of mythological volume '*Shiva Puraan*' in the present day context (Procreation, the Adorable); 01 commentary book on the first novel – 'A Pale View of the Hills' -- of the 2017 Nobel Literature laureate, Kazuo Ishiguro (Nagasaki: Bomb & Aftermath) are other books.

Not only an original writer as well as thinker, but also, a capable and versatile translator is '*Videh*' inasmuch as he has translated in English free verse form 02 *Hindee* poetry anthologies, viz. '*Hatyaaree Sadee Mein Jeevan Kee Khoj*' of '*Nirvikaar*' *Mukesh Kumaar,* and '*Adrishya Kaa Yathaarth*' of '*Ashwaghosh*' *Omprakaash Sharmaa* with the titles of the books being *seriatim* as 'Search for Life' and 'Reality of Invisible'.

The persona of '*Videh*' has been moulded by constant struggles and abject adversities, which have metamorphosed into his style of narration being quite frank as well as bland, if only straightforward.

His experiences of life are multifarious. He has not only suffered the pangs of extreme poverty and adversity in his childhood, but also, enjoyed the comforts and pleasures of the modern world by living in America. Besides, he has visited and toured in various foreign countries, too.

Not only in literature, but also, in exotic pursuits like meditation, spiritual practice, *Vipashyanaa, Yoga* practice, naturopathy, natural living, *Aarogya,* vegetarianism, gardening, tourism and long walks on foot *'Videh'* is equally active.

To add to his laurels, *'Videh'* has been honoured with their highest honour *'Shubham Ratna'* by the institution *'Shubham Saahitya, Kalaa Evam Sanskriti Sansthaan'* on the occasion of *Hindee Divas*, i.e. on 14th September, 2024.

The books of *'Videh'* are available in all the three formats, viz. eBooks, paperbacks and hardcovers from the Notion Press, Blue Rose One, Amazon and the Flipkart.

XXX

Table of Contents